THE STILLWATER GIRLS

OTHER TITLES BY MINKA KENT

The Thinnest Air

The Perfect Roommate

The Memory Watcher

THE STILLWATER GIRLS

MINKA KENT

This is a work of fiction. Names, characters, organizations, places, events, and incidents are either products of the author's imagination or are used fictitiously. Any resemblance to actual persons, living or dead, or actual events is purely coincidental.

Published by Thomas & Mercer, Seattle

www.apub.com

ISBN-13: 9781542044011 (hardcover)
ISBN-10: 1542044014 (hardcover)
ISBN-13: 9781542040105 (paperback)
ISBN-10: 1542040108 (paperback)

Cover design by Shasti O'Leary Soudant

Printed in the United States of America

First edition

For my darlings. And my darling.

CHAPTER 1

Wren

Sixty-three days—that's how long Mama's been gone. I drag my chalk against the blackboard, marking a jagged *X* across November twenty-first on our calendar.

Evie will be nine next Thursday—wherever she is.

I picture her crooked smile and blonde curls and knobby knees, and I smile to myself, but only for a second.

It takes a lot of energy to smile when your fingers are icicles and your stomach gnaws away at your insides and your eyelids are so heavy you can't see straight.

Lately Sage has taken to playing with the doll I sewed for Evie's birthday, even though at eighteen she's way too old for things like that. I suppose she finds comfort in having something to hold and rock the way Mama used to hold and rock her.

I don't need comfort.

I only need to survive.

The cabin's growing colder each night, and we've been taking turns waking up to stoke the fire. Last night, Sage forgot, and I woke up shivering with such force I could barely climb out of bed, and when I finally found the matches in the dark, my breath had turned to clouds.

I'd never known a cold like that before, one that rooted so far into my bones I thought they'd snap.

Tonight's wind howls, and Sage fixes breakfast eggs over a crackling fire, that scrappy doll resting in her chair with its dead button eyes, waiting.

We're always . . . waiting.

Meanwhile, supplies are dwindling, and we're weeks away from what I'm predicting will be a harsh winter. The ducks and geese migrated south earlier than normal this year, and the spiders are getting inside in droves, spinning enormous webs, which Mama always said was a sign.

We've lost five of our eight chickens in the past month, and we're not sure how or why. If Mama were here, she'd know. Every morning when we check the henhouse, I'm afraid I'm going to find another one lying lifeless on her side, being pecked at by some of the others. I don't want to think about what would happen if we lost the remaining three.

I wonder if they're sick like Evie.

And I wonder if she's still sick . . .

I assume so because we haven't so much as heard from Mama after they left in the middle of the night to get help for Evie, who was burning up and fighting to breathe, her chest rattling like pebbles in a tin can. The look in Mama's eyes as she wrapped our baby sister in wool blankets and packed a small bag is etched into my memory. I swear I can still see it clear as day every time I close my eyes.

Mama never panicked, but she panicked that night.

Her last words were, "Don't open the door for *anyone*, girls. You understand me?"

Mama's lips were thin and tight along her teeth as she spoke, and her eyes shook as she held my sister limp in her arms. A moment later, they left on foot, disappearing into the Stillwater Forest, which surrounds our homestead. With a galloping heart, I watched as Mama's pale dress turned dark in the distance and I could no longer see them anymore, and then I locked the door.

They should have been back by now.

CHAPTER 2

Nicolette

I'm in desperate need of a Band-Aid of the marital variety.

But Band-Aids aren't meant for gashes.

They're meant for little cuts and scrapes, hangnails and paper cuts—things that heal quickly before disappearing altogether. Our marriage is a jagged gash, all the good parts—the parts we need to survive and the parts that make us who we are together—gushing from the wound, and there's no tourniquet in sight.

I don't know how to stop the bleeding.

All I know is I have to try . . . because I'm losing him.

"They said we could schedule our home study whenever we want." I stand over the stove, sautéing garlic and kale in a Le Creuset pan as my husband glances up from his laptop at the kitchen table. "Won't be long, and we'll be licensed to foster in the state of New York."

Brant pushes his wire-frame glasses up the bridge of his straight nose, and I wait for a smile or a confirmation of some sort that this news is pleasing to him, but it never comes.

"They said it could take up to a year to get a placement once we're approved," I add, ignoring the guilt that comes in waves every time I sense my husband's void of excitement. "Or sometimes it happens right away. You just never know."

His attention returns to his screen, where he's elbow deep in photography edits for an upcoming exhibit. The Bellhaus Museum of Contemporary Art in Manhattan has chosen to showcase his work for the next four months. Despite the fact that it's been his lifelong dream to have his work honored and recognized by a world-renowned institution, he's been nothing but short-fused since we got the news.

I slide the limp kale and browned bits of garlic onto a serving dish with a wooden spoon and wipe my hands on my apron before checking on the roast chicken.

"Can you imagine kids running around in here?" I ask with a slight chuckle.

I can.

I've imagined it thousands of times before. Maybe more.

That's what happens when you meet the man of your dreams at twenty-two, marry him, postpone starting a family so you can travel the world by his side as he photographs the most beautiful things this earth has to offer, and then find your consciousness fading as you lie on an operating table for an emergency hysterectomy at the age of twenty-five.

"I don't need anyone but you, Nic. Never have, never will," Brant had told me as they wheeled me back that morning. He held my hand in his and pressed his lips against my fingers, his eyes resting on mine until my body was awash in warmth and his reassurance. It's the only thing I truly remember about that day. The rest is blurred and faded, washed away by years of trying to forget having a piece of my God-given womanhood ripped away without warning, without choice.

Turns out removing the ability to have babies does nothing to quell maternal urges. If anything, it only makes them less deniable, although the dream is that much more out of reach, placed on the top shelf with no stepladder in sight.

And speaking of dreams, I had another one of those baby dreams last night—the ones where I'm pushing a stroller around a park on a beautiful fall day, only when I glance down, I find my stroller empty.

It's always empty.

And it's always then that I wake up in a cold sweat, a gaping hollowness in my chest until I realize it wasn't real.

There's no baby. There never was.

My subconscious is a cruel, cowardly bitch that shows herself only when I'm unable to fight back, unable to shut her off.

I get it.

I'm empty.

I want something I can't have.

"You've edited those photos a hundred times already," I say, removing the chicken from our state-of-the-art oven in our state-of-the-art chef's kitchen, which happened to be a Christmas gift to ourselves two years ago. These are the things you get excited about when you don't have kids. But what I wouldn't give to be able to wipe sticky handprints off stainless steel just once.

Brant ignores my remark.

I ignore the sting of being in second place to his life's work.

It's always been this way, some years better or worse than others, but it's never been as bad as it has the past couple of years. At times, I find myself irrationally jealous of his work, as if she's a mistress who gives him everything he could ever want, which leaves me feeling inadequate and insecure, and I've never been that kind of person.

He says he has to chase his muse.

Sometimes that muse is me.

Sometimes it isn't.

I just miss his time, his present presence. I miss his laugh. His sweetness. His adoration. All the good parts, the parts I've loved with abandon, without question.

I miss *us*.

Plating his food, I carry our dinners to the table and take my seat beside him. With unabashed reluctance, he closes his laptop and pushes it aside.

"I'm so sorry, Nic." His hand reaches for mine, and our eyes meet as he exhales. "The Bellhaus exhibit is one of the greatest things to happen to me, and it's turning me into a self-centered ass."

He brings the top of my hand to his lips, and our gazes meet.

I bask in his unexpected moment of clarity, wrapping my bruised ego in it like a warm blanket. He gets it. For the first time in years, he finally gets it.

"I can't imagine the amount of pressure you're under," I say, ever the sympathetic partner. It's a part of me I can't shut off. "Just let me know what I can do to help, all right?"

I suppose I've created my own monster over the years, always supporting and understanding without a second thought, but that's what you do when you love someone, when you've promised to dedicate your entire life to them, come what may.

His happiness is mine and vice versa.

Or at least it used to be vice versa.

Brant lets me go and takes a fork from one of the folds of his cloth napkin. "So, this fostering thing . . ."

My stomach flips. Brant has never been the kind of man who yearned for children. Even from the beginning he had this take-it-or-leave-it attitude anytime I'd bring it up—always implying it was up to me.

After the hysterectomy, we looked into adoption, but we were told it could take upward of ten years to get a healthy infant, so we held off, convincing ourselves that we were enough for one another and justifying it every way we could.

"Maybe it's a sign," Brant had said at the time. "Not everyone's meant to be parents."

Brant dealt with our decision by burying himself in his work, accepting more international assignments and traveling every chance he got with me in tow. Seeing the world and escaping this one took my mind off the physical void that our decision left behind—but that was only temporary.

Eventually that void came back tenfold, and it always seems to worsen the colder the weather gets. Maybe it's the barren trees in the forest outside our home that trigger me. They look empty and dead this time of year—like my nonexistent womb.

I try not to think about the fact that we might have had a baby by now had we just stuck it out and placed ourselves on a waiting list.

Fear does that to you, though. It makes you question what you want and what you think you want.

"I hate not knowing what to expect, when we're going to be approved, and all that," I say, "but it's kind of exciting, right? It's like a little adventure."

"You're idealizing this," he says, like he's said a dozen times before, his tone gentle yet firm. "I just worry you'll get attached, and something will happen."

"I worry there's a child out there who needs us," I say. "So that worry overrides yours."

I wink to lighten my sentiment.

Brant smiles, lips closed as he chews, but his eyes crinkle at the corners, squinting as he loses himself in thought. Having been with this man the better part of my entire adult life, I can almost surmise what he's thinking.

Will you be okay at home alone with the child while I travel?

Will you miss seeing the world with me?

Do you fully understand everything you're giving up to do this?

What if we can't bond with the child?

What if the child has issues we're not equipped to handle?

If he were to ask me these things, as he has in the past, I'd give him the same, unchanged answer: he needs to leave the worrying to me.

There isn't a single scenario I haven't spent hours hashing out in my mind whenever I'm struck by a sleepless night—which lately has been far too often since Brant holes himself up in his studio until the wee hours of the morning, finishing his latest commissioned project for *Vanity Fair*.

My husband turns his attention to his dinner, drawing into his introverted shell all over again, and I think about the thing I've been trying not to think about since the moment I came across it in his sock drawer.

We need a tourniquet, and we need one now because I'm losing him.

CHAPTER 3

WREN

I would do anything to know simplicity the way Sage does.

My stomach won't stop rumbling, my head won't stop pounding, and Sage won't stop singing.

I'm two seconds from snapping at the only person I have any control over until I force the thought away and make my way to the small window in the kitchen. I gaze past a checkered curtain toward the forest, as I've done many times before. The tiniest piece of me hopes Mama and Evie will emerge out of thin air, running for the house with exhausted smiles on their faces, home from their perilous journey at last.

Every night as I lie in bed, I picture the two of them coming home, and I wake with dried tears on my pillows. I've never been much for mollycoddling like Sage is, but lately my patience is worn thin by the end of the evening.

It isn't the only thing wearing thin these days, though.

My hope.

My body.

Our supplies.

This life.

Everything's just . . . dwindling into nothing.

Pretty soon there'll be nothing left.

The thought of wasting away, freezing and starving to death with my naive little sister, makes my stomach twist in knots, but the thought of leaving the homestead and going beyond the forest sends my heart slamming to the ground.

We're not allowed to go past the forest, and even if we did venture that way, we wouldn't know where to go. We'd likely get picked off by some hungry coyote.

If I'm going to die, I'd rather die here, beside the sooty fireplace that's kept us warm and cooked our meals and hosted hundreds upon hundreds of Mama's beloved story hours. I'd rather die with my tattered books and sketch pads and the collection of dolls I've sewn my younger sisters over the years. I'd rather die wrapped in one of Mama's old dresses and breathing in the scent of her lavender goat's-milk soap than lying in an earthen bed, covered in snapped twigs and broken leaves.

"Sage. Enough." My voice cutting through the cabin startles her into silence. Maybe I should let her sing, maybe it fills her with what little joy she can find, but it's nightfall now, and the sooner we can go to bed, the sooner we get a break from this never-ending day, and the sooner we won't have to feel so hungry, so tired, so alone.

Heading to the door, I secure the latch and draw the curtains on the little window, as we always do at sundown.

"Bad things happen at night," Mama always warned us. *"People feel emboldened to do the kinds of things they'd never be caught dead doing in the light of day."*

She never did say what those things were. I didn't want to know—but I could only imagine.

"The world's an evil place, my darlings," she would say as she brushed the hair off our foreheads and kissed our chubby, soap-scented cheeks at night. *"You're safe here. With me. I'll never let anything happen to you."*

The fireplace crackles, and a quiet Sage rocks in a chair, the baby doll tucked tight under one arm as she leans down to study a puzzle piece in the dim firelight.

I change behind the wardrobe door in the corner of the room, my dress crumpling to the floor. Pulling one of Mama's old nightdresses over my head, I tug it down my bony hips until the lace hem tickles the tops of my feet. Sweeping my hands beneath my thick hair, I tie it low at the nape of my neck before heading to the basin to wash up.

An old canning jar filled with toothbrushes rests beside the day's water, and I pluck mine—a garish shade of neon green. It's always been funny to me that everything around us is white or cream or brown or gray—beautifully dull—but these are wonderfully bright, like the box of waxy colored sticks Mama got for Evie on her fifth birthday.

The Man—the one Mama meets every few months to get our supplies—picked them up for her. She didn't say where he got them, but she did say there are shops and places that sell these sorts of things, just like there are places that sell the feed we give our chickens and goats and the fabric and thread we use to make our clothes.

I once asked Mama if she could take me to a shop someday so I could pick out a new dress pattern or some kind of fabric that wasn't covered in tiny flowers, but her eyes began to water, and she answered by telling me to peel the dinner potatoes and humming "Simple Gifts" under her breath.

I loved Mama too much to upset her, and I respected Mama too much to ever bring it up again.

Gathering my nightdress in my hands, I lower myself to the warm flames in the hearth beside my silent sister and stoke the dying fire. I add three more logs, which should get us through the next several hours, and then I pad across the wooden floor to my bed in the corner, slipping into my warmest pair of wool socks.

"You should wash up," I say, climbing beneath Mama's favorite quilt a moment later.

Sage reaches for another puzzle piece, yawning. "I'm not tired."

"Right." Rolling my eyes, I add, "Fine. Suit yourself."

Sage snaps her piece into place before exhaling. "They're not coming back, are they?"

Sitting up, I pull the covers to my waist and contemplate my answer.

"How long has it been, Wren?" she asks.

I shouldn't be surprised that I'm the only one counting days. Sage doesn't know what month it is half the time, and why should she? I've always been the keeper of the calendar. She's only ever had to wash supper dishes and gather eggs and flash her tender grin to get out of everything else.

"It's been . . . a while." I don't tell her it's been seventy-three days as of tonight.

"Mama would've sent for us by now, don't you think?" She turns to me, clutching that ridiculous rag doll against her chest like a girl half her age.

"No one's ever been here before. Who would she send?"

Sage lifts a bony shoulder to her ear, her dark, pin-straight hair settling into her hollow clavicles. "I don't know . . . The Man?"

"How would he know how to find us?" I've asked myself these same questions, silently, over the past several weeks, always coming to the same conclusions. Mama's always made sure no one knew where we were. Every time she'd meet The Man, she'd be gone at least eight hours or more, wheeling everything back in two separate red wagons, and she'd never let us help. Sage wasn't strong enough to make the journey, and Mama needed me to stay home to look after Evie. Besides, it wasn't safe for young girls to be in the woods after dark.

There were too many things that could happen to us in the forest—men with guns, rabid animals, I always assumed, though I've never seen either of those things in my nearly twenty years on this earth.

My sister doesn't answer as she rocks her baby doll and watches as the flames lick the inside of the hearth.

Lying back, I bring the covers to my neck and roll to my side, my heavy eyelids drifting shut.

"Do you think something happened to them?" Sage asks when I'm halfway asleep.

My brows knit, though my eyes remain closed. "Sage. Go to bed. Please. We'll talk in the morning."

The creak of the rocking chair fills the small cabin, and the soft crumpled sound of the rag doll hitting the floor follows.

"I need to use the outhouse," she announces, voice small because she knows she waited too long.

It takes all the energy I have to roll over, and when I open my eyes, I discover my sister standing in front of my bed with wincing, desperate eyes.

"I've already locked up for the night. You couldn't have gone earlier?" I ask.

"I *really* have to go." She bites her lower lip, bouncing in place as her hands cup her privates through her dress. "I'm going to wet myself."

Flinging the covers off my legs, I step out of bed. For as long as I can remember, Sage has had issues with her bladder. When she was a young girl, she used to ignore her urges too long and then cry every time she peed, saying it burned, which would only make her hold it in even longer. Mama started ordering antibiotic tablets from The Man after that.

We ran out last month.

Slipping my hand around hers, I grab our jackets off the hooks by the door and light the kerosene lamp before checking the window and working the latch. Under the shade of night and a moonless sky, we dash across the sod, past the goat enclosure, between the henhouse and the garden shed, and at last, to the leaning outhouse on the perimeter of the homestead.

"Be quick," I tell her, catching the door as she flings it open. Wrapping my arms around my body, I struggle to get warm as the chilly air bites through my coat and works its way into the thin fabric of my nightdress. With chattering teeth, I ask if she's finished yet.

"Almost," she calls.

Stepping to the south side of the outhouse in hopes to avoid the cruel north wind, I peer toward the darkened Stillwater Forest, toward the same little clearing Mama and Evie disappeared into seventy-three nights ago.

Had I known it would be the last time I'd ever see them, I might have told them I loved them one more time. I might have kissed Evie's chubby little fingers and hugged Mama so tight she'd have had to pry me off her just to breathe again.

I'd have thanked Mama for everything. For her protection from the evils of the world. For the hot meals, warm clothes, and shelter from the cold. For the joyful songs and heartfelt lullabies. For the books that fed my mind and allowed me to escape to other worlds on those endless summer days. For the stories of her beautiful childhood, when the world was a kinder, sweeter place, and the tales of all the family members we were never able to meet before the outside world had turned greedy and cold.

But mostly, I'd have thanked her for her unconditional love.

The door to the outhouse creaks open before the wind catches it and bangs it against the side of the little building.

"Wren?" Sage calls for me.

"Over here." I step out from the south side of the outhouse and take her hand, leading her back to our house, where the warm glow of the fire through the windows lights the way. "Feel better?"

She nods.

"You'll go to bed now?" I ask.

Sage nods again.

"I promise we'll talk in the morning," I say once we're halfway to the door. I'm not sure what I can tell her to calm her concerns when I've spent weeks trying—and failing—to calm my own, but I'll try my best to ensure I don't steal what hope remains from those sweet, coffee-colored eyes.

As soon as we're inside, I hang our coats, and Sage changes into her nightgown, a white cotton dress with a lace hem that once belonged to me, and I watch as she slips an extra pair of gray woolen socks over the ones she already wears.

I lock the door for the final time this evening, shutting out the silence that reminds me of how alone we truly are in this world—and in this land Mama always called "our little slice of heaven on earth" and "the place where no one can ever hurt us."

Grabbing Sage's doll from the floor, I place it on the pillow beside her, promising myself I'll be better tomorrow. Maybe I'll sing her one of Mama's favorite songs and try to find a way to distract her from all this, if only for moments at a time.

"I won't let anything happen to us," I tell her, tucking her into bed a second later and kissing her forehead the way Mama always did. "I promise."

Returning to my bed and burrowing under my quilt, I draw the covers over my head and take comfort in what body heat I have left.

We're not going to die.

Not here.

Not like this.

Not cold and alone and forgotten.

Mama wouldn't want that for her darlings.

CHAPTER 4

Nicolette

"I thought *I* was supposed to be the nervous one tonight." Brant places his hand on the small of my back and hands me a champagne flute.

Offering a hesitant smile, I begin to respond, but he's ushered away by some man in a three-piece suit and a woman in head-to-toe diamonds and Givenchy.

Everyone here tonight is a buyer, a dealer, or a faithful lover of the photographic arts, and one person here tonight, I presume, is a lover of my husband.

"Nicolette? My God, it's been forever." An old colleague of mine from the Berkshire Gallery years ago strides toward me, placing her hand on my arm and kissing the air beside my left cheek.

Her name doesn't come to me immediately because I knew her a lifetime ago and only briefly. I hadn't worked there very long when a handsome photographer came in for a meeting with the director and left with my personal cell number and the promise of drinks the following Friday.

M . . . her name starts with an *M*.

Mariah . . . Marie . . . Marin.

That's it.

"Marin," I say, recycling the same manufactured excitement I've been using all evening. "So lovely to see you. Glad you could make it."

Her manicured hand splays across her freckled décolletage. "Brant Gideon and the Bellhaus Museum? Are you kidding me? I wouldn't have missed it for the world. This is huge. I remember when he was just starting out. Hottest starving artist I'd ever laid eyes on . . . and then you just had to walk in and steal him from me."

Marin bats my arm.

"You know I'm kidding," she says, head tilted as her smile fades. "You two are disgustingly perfect for each other, and I couldn't be happier for you. Anyway, heard you two left the city. Where are you these days?"

I sip my champagne, letting the bubbles tickle my throat before I answer. "Upstate."

Marin studies me, her busy eyes narrowing. "Huh. Didn't expect that."

Lifting a brow, I ask, "Really?"

She shrugs. "I just figured it'd be someplace a little more . . . exotic? Given his profession."

"We travel, but he likes the solitude," I say, "when he's not shooting."

"But do *you*?"

I hesitate. Her question is a bit invasive considering she hasn't seen me since I was twenty-two.

"I'm sorry," she says, waving her hand. "I just . . . I remember when we worked together, and you always said you wanted an apartment overlooking Central Park. I believe you said you were born and raised in the city, and you were going to die here, too."

Yes. I did say that. I'd completely forgotten.

I smirk, raising my flute. "They say if you want to make God laugh, just tell him your plans, right?"

Marin chuckles, though I didn't think my comment was that funny, and then I catch her glance toward my husband.

"Anyway, I should make my rounds," she says, swatting my wrist. "I'm only here to network. And to ogle your husband."

Marin winks before she struts away, and I begin to recall her odd sense of humor and the fact that I never could tell when she was serious and when she was joking.

I let it go. Marin's hardly a threat. She isn't his type in the least.

She was always loud. And she name-dropped in nearly every conversation I ever had with her. Brant was never about status and social climbing—that's what I loved about him when we first met. He genuinely had no idea who my parents were, and that placed him a notch above every other man I'd ever met.

Standing in a room of recognizable strangers, a veritable who's who of the Manhattan art scene, I watch as every eye manages to land on my husband, who steps out of his introverted shell and dons the charismatic suit of a larger-than-life artistic visionary. People circle around him, clinging to his every word as if he's sharing the most fascinating things they've ever heard.

He gifts them with warm smiles and the occasional handshake, and he leads a group of them around, elaborating on his inspiration behind his "Lost in Nature" series—the passion project he's been working on since we moved away from the city.

This is his life's work, and it's inventive and breathtaking.

I just didn't think it was going to be almost a decade in the making.

Scanning the room, I find a portrait he took of me, standing barefoot in a brook, the sunrise kissing the top of my head as I gather my sheer dress in my hand. A woman in a slinky black number saunters up to it, alone, a glass of red wine in her hand and a diamond tennis bracelet hanging from her left wrist.

She studies my photo.

I study her.

The woman lingers in front of the picture a little longer before strutting toward the next one—an eerie photo of a forest clearing at dawn—but she doesn't stay there long before moving to the next and the next. But after a few minutes, she returns to the one of me.

I'm glued. I couldn't look away from her if I tried.

Is she the one?

Is this the woman my husband was seeing? The woman he might have fathered a child with?

Is she scoping me out the way a mistress would compare herself to her lover's wife?

Her onyx hair creates a shiny curtain, hiding part of her face, the ends cut blunt. She's stunning in a serious, intelligent, upper-class New York kind of way, oozing elegance and grace from every angle.

I'm not sure how long I've been watching her study my photograph, but my heart slams on the floor and my blood runs cold when I spot my husband approaching her.

She smiles the second they lock eyes, and he leans in, kissing the space between her mouth and cheek—not just the air beside it. He touches her bare arm as they speak, and his eyes are wide and expressive with every word. It's as if no one exists but her.

He's absolutely besotted.

And I recognize the look she's giving him—it's the very same look I gave him when I was a young butterfly thrilled to be caught in his net.

A couple of guests squeeze past them, forcing Brant to step closer to the woman to let them pass.

He doesn't move back, though.

He just stays, comfortable in her personal space like he knows her well.

The champagne bubbles in my stomach become unsettled, and I glance around for the nearest ladies' room in case I'm going to be sick.

Brant is charming, I'll give him that. And he's warm and personable. But of all the exhibits and gallery openings and book signings we've attended, I've never seen him behave with anyone the way he's behaving with this woman.

I swear his dimples grow deeper by the second, and there's a distinct twinkle in his sea-green eyes so noticeable I can see it from all the way over here.

"You okay?" A warm palm finds my shoulder, and I glance over to see Marin standing next to me. "You look like you're going to be sick."

I force a smile and shake my head. "This champagne. I don't think it's agreeing with me."

Her brows rise, and she laughs through her nose. "Sweetie, it's *Cristal.* Cristal agrees with *everyone*. Sure you're okay?"

Brant and the woman are still lost in their little conversation, though at this point they might as well be lost in their own little world.

My blood, which was ice-cold a moment ago, is now hot, burning beneath the surface of my skin. If I wasn't a proper lady, I'd have half a mind to capture his attention and ask him what the hell is going on.

But I won't do that here. I won't make a scene in front of the people who could make or break the future of the career he's worked for his entire life.

Marin follows my gaze, quickly piecing together the thing I refuse to say out loud.

"That woman with the dark hair?" Marin nods in their direction. "She's a photographer. Her style is pretty similar to Brant's. I think she's just a huge fan. Comes into Berkshire all the time trying to get us to broker her work."

"What's her name?" This might be my one and only chance to find out.

"Clara Briese," she says.

I burn the name into my mind, silently reciting it dozens of times in case I ever need to know it in the future.

"She was staring at my picture earlier," I say, though I'm not sure why I'm admitting this to Marin or if it even means anything. Breathing life into that observation makes it seem like a silly thing to get worked up about.

Marin chuckles. "She probably thinks you're beautiful."

In the quiet of my mind, I write off her explanation as too simplistic and optimistic to quell my concern.

"She dates women," Marin adds. "And only women. Anyway, here comes trouble." She moved back into the crowd.

I glance past her to find my husband headed in my direction.

"You doing okay?" he asks when he arrives at my side. I choke on the familiar cologne that invades my lungs, the same sensual, woodsy cologne that once brought me comfort because it smelled like home.

Smiling, I offer a quick nod because I'm more okay than I was five minutes ago. "Of course. You?"

"Of course."

My husband examines me.

"If you're not feeling well, just say so," he says. "We'll leave right away."

"Don't be ridiculous. This is your night. And I'm fine," I lie.

Brant's face lights, though not half as brightly as it lit for Clara. At least I know now that *he's* not *her* type.

"You know, this night is beautiful, and it's been a long time coming," he says, "but I can't stop thinking about how the most exquisite thing in this room is standing right here in front of me."

He leans in, his lips grazing mine as his fingers lightly trace the side of my cheek.

"You're not just my muse," he says. "You're my *everything*. None of this would've been possible without you."

A year ago, I'd have believed him—as I always have.

But after finding the photograph of a towheaded little girl with Brant's sea-green eyes hiding beneath the leather organizer tray of his sock drawer last month, I don't know that I can.

Brant kisses me once more before dragging the tips of his fingers down my arm and stopping to give my hand a squeeze. "Moffatt just walked in, and his pockets are looking a little heavy. Should probably say hello . . ."

He smiles at me, expecting a knowing chuckle, which I force myself to give him, and my chest tightens.

Extending his bent arm, he nods. "Come with me. I'll introduce you."

I've spent the majority of my adult life following this man through Moroccan souks and over Grecian cliffs, through ancient Mayan ruins and lush Amazonian paradises. I left Manhattan—the only *home* I'd ever known—because he asked me to. And then I made us our own little domestic nirvana in his depressing, hole-in-the-wall hometown of Stillwater Hills, New York, ignoring the gnawing homesickness that never quite passed. I cooked his favorite gourmet meals each night and learned to like his beloved jazz standards. I made love to him when I sensed he needed a release, even if I wasn't exactly in the mood myself. I brought him coffee when he pulled all-nighters, and I massaged his shoulders when he'd spent too many hours hunched over his computer, knee-deep in edits.

But the one and only thing I could never give him was a family.

It kills me that someone else may have.

Slinking my arm into his and burying my unease, I feel like a fraud as he introduces me to real estate mogul Robert Moffatt and his stunning young wife, pedigreed and pregnant socialite Temple Rothschild-Moffatt, who clearly hasn't let her third trimester keep her from dressing in head-to-toe Versace and six-inch stilettos.

Brant and Robert's conversation fades to the background, and Temple excuses herself as I scan the gallery once more, my gaze landing on every pretty face in the room.

The cigarette-thin blonde with the faux fur stole.

The bookish brunette with the red-painted lips and clear-frame glasses.

The lavender-haired socialite who steals glances at my husband when she thinks no one's watching.

It could be any of them.

And it could be none of them at all.

The only thing I know for sure is that needing to know exactly who she is is beginning to consume my every thought.

Brant's hand slips to the small of my back, and he pulls me closer. The room spins, my breath shortens, and a prickle of sweat collects across my brow.

"Excuse me," I say, interrupting their conversation and showing myself outside. I've never had a panic attack before, but I'm quite certain I'm standing at the water's edge of my first one.

It's mid-December, and the sidewalks are dusted with powdery snow. A few nearby shops are closed for the evening, but their holiday lights flicker in the windows, and holly wreaths hang on their glass doors. These things used to send a blanket of warmth cascading through me when I'd see them.

Now I feel nothing.

Gasping for air, I close my eyes and try to focus on the sensation of the chilled air in my lungs, and then I count backward from ten, telling myself that when I get to one, I'm going to be fine . . . at least for now.

Ten . . .

Nine . . .

Eight . . .

Seven . . .

"Nicolette."

I open my eyes to find my husband standing outside the door to the museum, his hands shoved in the pockets of his Prada suit. The casualness in his pose is an insult.

"Talk to me," he says before he strides toward me, head cocked ever so slightly. He looks at me like I'm an impossible riddle he can't quite solve. "You're not you, and you haven't been all night."

My lips part in response, but I don't know what to tell him.

I'm still trying to figure out where to go from here—when to confront him, how to confront him, not to mention how I'm supposed to feel given the fact that I've conjured up some worst-case scenario over a single photograph.

Brant wraps his arms around me, the warmth of his body and heaviness of his hold equally comforting and suffocating.

"If you don't mind," I say, my voice muffled against his pristine suit jacket, "I'm going to catch a cab back to the hotel. I think I'm coming down with something."

He pulls away, and his eyes rest on mine. Again, he doesn't believe me, but at this point I don't care. All I can think about is peeling myself out of this dress, yanking the bobby pins from my hair, and washing the makeup from my face before tears have a chance to ruin it.

Everything else I can deal with another time, when I haven't had three glasses of champagne and unraveled myself all because a beautiful woman was staring at my photo for too long and then my husband greeted her with his signature dimpled smile and sparkling-green gaze.

Brant peers over my shoulder toward a set of oncoming headlights and lifts his arm to hail the taxi.

"Get some rest," he says, gathering the train of my dress and helping me in. Closing the door, he motions for me to lower the window. "I'll have my phone on if you need anything."

I appreciate his concern, but I can't deny the tiniest voice in the back of my head telling me how strange it is for him to send me off without a second thought.

Taking my hand from his, I give him a small wave, catching the glint of his eyes as they reflect in the full moon above. Once upon a time, those eyes felt like home every time I looked into them.

Now all I see is that little girl.

CHAPTER 5

Wren

"Wren, it *snowed*." Sage wakes me with an eager squeal, and I pull my covers back over my head. "Can we make snow candy?"

I don't have the energy to tell her we need molasses for snow candy and we don't have molasses.

Nor do we have sugar.

We don't have anything besides eggs and goat's milk; one last bag of flour; some canned beans; and a few potatoes, onions, and garlic in the root cellar.

I took inventory yesterday, something I'd been dreading for weeks. But it had to be done.

Getting out of bed and stepping into my boots, I tighten the laces before grabbing my winter coat from the back of the door and the egg basket by the front door. I need to check on the hens to make sure they made it through last night's cold snap.

"I'll be back," I tell Sage.

Trudging through the snow, which almost covers the top of my boots, I'm halfway to the henhouse when my tired eyes are pulled to a set of tracks cutting across the front yard and leading around the house.

Stopping, I hunch down to examine them closer.

Boots.

They're boot prints. And they're huge.

Dropping the basket, I sprint back to the cabin, slipping through melting slush the entire way, and once inside, I slam the door, unable to lock it fast enough.

"Wren? What's wrong?" Sage comes to my side, but I hurry across the room and grab a chair, bringing it back to the door.

Climbing on the seat, I reach for the shotgun perched above the door.

"Wren." Sage says my name harder this time, her chest rising and falling almost faster than my own. "What are you doing? You're scaring me."

"Footprints," I say, breathless and light-headed as the room around me spins. "There were footprints outside."

"Coyote? Bear? What?" she asks.

"Boots. Big boots."

Sage goes to the window by the door, drawing back the curtain a few inches and peeking outside, but I pull her away.

Mama told us it's every man for themselves out there, and we all have to do what we all have to do in order to survive. She assured us we were safe here, calling our home a fortress, which I always thought was silly because all it took was a good hailstorm or some strong winds, and water and wind would find their way in.

If the elements could get in, so could anyone or anything else.

Racking the shotgun, I rest it on my shoulder and reach for the doorknob.

"What are you doing?" Sage asks. Her glassy eyes shine like two polished marbles.

"I'm going to follow the tracks." I ignore the hard knot in my throat that makes it difficult to swallow and the tremble in my hands as I grip the gun. I'll inspect the perimeter of the homestead, but I suspect the man's gone now, and I expect his tracks to lead into the forest, where I'll have to stop.

But if he's out there, hiding, and he sees me with a gun, maybe he won't come back again.

Heading outside with my heart in my teeth and the butt of my shotgun tucked tight beneath my arm, I follow the boot prints in the snow, the crunch of my own boots and the bleats of our goats filling my ears.

I don't know who he is or what he wants, but I won't hide like a coward.

I won't be a sitting duck.

CHAPTER 6

NICOLETTE

The child in the grocery cart in front of me kicks his mother, and I watch as she reaches for his legs, gripping them and holding them down. He squirms. She whispers something in his ear. He pouts. She carries on, pushing her cart toward the end of the aisle.

I'm sure this scene plays out in every grocery store across America, but I'm caught in this moment, watching the two of them in real time and inserting myself in her place.

The mother's yoga pants are covered in flecks of golden dog hair and her T-shirt is wrinkled, but her dark hair is piled into a shiny ballerina bun on the top of her head, and when she turns to the side, I catch her profile.

She's pretty, even with the dark circles under her eyes and the youthfulness filling out her baby face. A thin gold band rests on her left ring finger, accented by the tiniest diamond.

My hands grip the handle of the cart, and I peel my gaze off the two of them as I try to remember what I needed from this aisle. Almond flour? Xylitol? Sugar-free dark chocolate baking bits? These aren't my usual staples, but Brant is on some sugar-free, paleo, gluten-free something-or-other fad diet that he is convinced sharpens his creative acumen.

I rack my mind, drawing blank after blank.

The lack of sleep these last few weeks is taking a toll on my short-term memory. I tried melatonin tablets for a few weeks, but those only gave me nightmares—very specific nightmares involving my husband, the blonde child, and the faceless other woman.

In the middle of a small-town grocery store, I entertain the fact that I could be wrong about all this—and I hope to God that I am.

For years, I've had these silly little reveries of this fictional family of ours. Daydreams of my husband snapping pictures of our child that I lovingly arrange in albums, road trips to my parents' house in Nantucket, where they greet our little one with open arms and twirling hugs, where Mom teaches them how to bake her famous raspberry-oatmeal cookies and Dad teaches them how to sail on his beloved *Parsival III*. I've envisioned ski trips to Vermont and European summer vacations, and I've prayed for late-morning pancake breakfasts and back-to-school shopping excursions to the city.

If I'm lucky, all is not lost.

And if I'm not, I've wasted years on woolgathering and dandelion wishes.

He'd been pulling away for the past year, and all that time I assumed it was because things were getting tired and stale between us. I assumed we needed to embark on a new chapter in our lives, and I was convinced we were ready.

So I pushed for us to become foster parents.

Baby steps, I'd called it. And I'd pushed hard and in my own way, the way a desperate woman would, dropping hints and batting lashes and making jokes that were never fully jokes at all.

It took a while for Brant to warm up to the idea, and I blamed his reluctance at the time on his upcoming travel schedule. When he finally agreed, I credited his acceptance to his guilt over his disproportioned work-life balance and the fact that I'd never asked for anything of him, ever.

Now I fear he's simply biding his time, waiting for the perfect opportunity to shatter my heart and burn our life together to the ground. Only I'm not sure what his plan is . . . because he's the one with the fame, but I'm the one with the money.

The house. The cars. I bought them all with family money from my trust fund. Brant makes a healthy income on his own, I'll give him that, but without me, his standard of living would take a noticeable hit. Not to mention, you can't put a price on never having to worry about money a day in your life.

As far as I know, Brant hasn't saved a single penny of his earnings, but mostly because he didn't need to. Our future is set, at least financially. We always treated his income as fun money, money he could spend on anything he pleased because he earned it and we didn't necessarily need it.

If that child truly is his, I imagine much of his earnings are going to the girl's mother these days.

Up ahead, the exhausted woman with the tired toddler must feel my stare, because without warning, she careens her body toward mine, her eyes tightening when we lock gazes.

This isn't an uncommon occurrence for me.

I've been an "outsider" ever since we moved here. Doesn't matter that I've lived here for over a decade, I'm still just that "rich bitch who lives outside of town." People see me with my curated, wrinkle-free outfits and French designer handbags, they see the lack of worry lines on my forehead, the lack of bags under my eyes, and they think I have it all.

Once upon a not-so-distant time . . . I did.

I offer a smile, and her expression softens when she realizes I'm not judging her, that I'm not as unapproachable as I seem. And if I wouldn't come off as some kind of overly personal weirdo, I'd tell her how lucky she is to wear leggings and topknots each day and to get to vacuum crushed goldfish crackers from the crevices of her minivan seats and plan easy, kid-friendly menus.

What I wouldn't give to have a taste of an exhaustion so meaningful.

Turning away and repositioning her body, she blocks the sight line between myself and her child—as if I'm not welcome to look at him any longer—and I get it now. She thought I was staring at her child.

Years ago—long before we moved here—there were a couple of kidnappings in the town, both of them babies and both of them snatched in broad daylight. The locals never got over the fear, never got over the trauma of knowing something evil lurked in their precious Stillwater Hills. A slew of families even moved away, driven out by the fear of not knowing which child would be next.

I don't blame any mother who tries to protect her child.

It's her right, her duty.

"He's adorable," I say as I push my cart past her and her blue-eyed boy, hoping to subtly let her know I'm not a threat in the least.

"Thank you," she says, her voice breathy as she moves her cart out of the way.

Coconut flour.

That's what I needed.

I grab a one-pound bag off a shelf and make my way to the meat counter to check a few more items off my list before I head home, start dinner, and do my best to pretend everything is fine and that I'm not slowly unraveling.

One thread pull, and I'd be bare.

And I'm not quite sure what that would mean, but it can't possibly be good for either of us.

CHAPTER 7

Wren

The snow lasted all of twenty-four hours before melting like it was never there at all. I suppose the ground was too warm to sustain it. I'm normally not sorry to see it go, but in this case, we've lost our only ability to know if that man comes back here again.

Wrapped in my jacket and laced boots, I tuck the shotgun under my arm and head to the chicken coop. As far as I can tell, there aren't any new tracks or anything out of place or amiss.

Doesn't keep my heart from drumming or my breaths from turning shallow.

Heading into the henhouse, I lean the gun against one of the walls and stop in my tracks when I find one of our Rhode Island Reds lying motionless on the ground. Dropping to her level, I place my hand on her feathered wing.

She's still warm.

I try to move her, gently rocking her back and forth, but her eyes stay closed. The two remaining hens, two White Leghorns that we've had the longest, cluck around me, flapping their wings as if they know something is wrong.

Placing my palm along her body again, I determine she isn't breathing.

My lip begins to quiver, but I bite it until I taste blood and the threat of tears goes away. Mama always warned us about getting attached to livestock, but I loved this silly little hen. She was the friendliest of the bunch, and when we'd let them out to roam, she'd follow me like a second shadow. She'd even eat out of my hand if I offered.

I'd never told anyone, but I named her Ruby.

It was our little secret.

Scooping her into my arms, I carry her outside and place her body next to a leafless shade tree before heading to the garden shed to grab a shovel. The earth will be hard and cold, but I need to bury her body so we don't attract any predators.

If she hadn't died from an unknown illness, we could eat her, and then she wouldn't have died for nothing, but it isn't safe for us.

A half hour later, I've scooped the final mound of dirt over Ruby, prickles of sweat tickling my skin beneath my layers of clothing. My fingertips are ice and my body is fire, and despite the fact that I've only been up an hour, I would give anything to go back to bed already.

With shaky arms, I lean the shovel against the tree and stumble inside, closing the door and taking a second to rest against it as I catch my breath and let the heat of the fire warm the ice-cold tip of my nose.

"What's wrong?" Sage asks. "And where are the eggs?"

Peeling my coat from my shoulders, I hang it on the hook before bending down to tug on the lace of my left boot. "We lost another one."

Sage says nothing. She knows there's nothing we can do to stop it if we don't know what's causing it. I don't want to think about what's going to happen if we lose one more. Our hens each lay an egg a day, and we need those eggs.

"Wren?" Sage asks, her big eyes flicking to mine.

"Yeah?"

"Will you play checkers with me?"

I begin to protest but stop. We used to play checkers all the time, and now I can't remember the last time we played anything. Besides, I don't think Sage is wanting to play checkers so much as she's wanting a moment for things to feel normal again.

Grabbing the box off the shelf in the corner, I take it to the kitchen table and flash a smile. My sister jumps up from her chair and meets me at the table, sliding into her seat with a grin on her face.

"I'm red," she says, helping me set up the board, "so you can go first."

Pushing a black checker to a new square, I sit back and watch my sister contemplate her next move. It isn't until my next turn that I realize I've bitten my nails to the quick, and I have no recollection of doing so.

"Your turn," I say, tucking my ugly hands out of sight.

Sage stares out the window beside us, her body motionless, like one of those Greek statues I've seen in Mama's book of Greek art and archaeology.

"Do you hear that, Wren?" Her voice is the softest whisper.

The hair on the back of my neck stands on end despite the fact that I don't hear a thing but the howl of the wind and the occasional bleat of a goat.

"What's it sound li—"

"Shh!" Sage lifts a finger, her gaze shifting as she scans the section of land visible from here.

The snap of twigs and footsteps shuffling through soggy dead leaves outside our cabin force the two of us to lock gazes and hold our breath.

"Wren. The gun . . ." Sage points to the empty rack above the door, and my heart sinks.

"I left it in the henhouse," I whisper.

Three swift raps on the door echo through our cabin. Sage claps her hands over her nose and mouth, and I don't move a muscle. The only kind of weapons we have in here are kitchen utensils, and last I checked, our butcher knives were in dire need of sharpening.

The person on the other side of the door knocks again.

Three times again.

Sage begins to rise, like she's lost her mind and wants to answer the door, but I lean across the table and grab her by the wrists. Her brows furrow, and she yanks away from my unsteady grip.

"Wren!" she says, her soft voice barely audible.

"Quiet," I tell her in a whispered yell, lifting my palm.

"What if it's Mama?" she asks, ignoring me.

I swallow the lump in my throat. "Mama wouldn't knock."

CHAPTER 8

Nicolette

"It's a shame Brant wasn't able to join us tonight." My mother plunges her fork into a slice of her birthday cake with as much grace as a true Preston can, and she cups the underside of her utensil as she brings it in for another bite.

"He sends his love," I say. "And you'll see him first thing in the morning."

"This cake is to die for. He's really missing out." Mom points at the white-frosted confection with the tines of her fork.

I wave her comment away with my hand. "He's on this sugar-free, gluten-free thing right now. This would be torture for him."

Every year, the weekend before Christmas, my parents drive from their second home in Nantucket to Stillwater Hills to spend a couple of days with us, doubling down for my mother's birthday and the holidays before I leave to finish out the rest of winter with my best friend in Florida. It's been this way for the entirety of our marriage, so I find it odd that Brant committed himself to work obligations on this particular evening.

And he and my father are practically best friends, my dad bragging to his yacht club cronies and anyone else who'll listen that Brant is the son-in-law he always hoped to have.

Brant isn't quite so vocally braggadocian, but I know the feeling is mutual. His father left their family when he and his younger brother, Davis, were barely out of diapers. His mom spent the majority of their childhood drunk or high, sometimes drunk *and* high.

My parents are the only family he has that truly love and cherish him the way he always wanted to be loved and cherished. They're the only family he really has anymore. His mother passed away shortly after we married—cirrhosis of the liver—and his brother lives in a decrepit trailer on the far side of Stillwater Hills, working nights at the tire factory and spending most of his free time at the strip club in the next town over.

"Where'd you say Brant was tonight?" Dad asks.

"Speaking engagement," I say.

"What kind of speaking engagement?" he asks. It isn't like my father to pry about details, so his question catches me off guard.

The truth is . . . I don't know. I don't have an answer for him.

Brant claims he's speaking at some members-only, country club charity function tonight in Albany, and when I asked if he wanted me to tag along—for moral support . . . as I've always done—he insisted I stay here and wait for my parents to arrive.

I couldn't even tell them what he's speaking about, and not once did I see him practice.

"You'll have to ask him when you see him tomorrow." Ignoring the heavy tightness in the pit of my stomach, I top off my wineglass. "So how's the Carlton Hotels buyout going?"

"Couldn't be better. First of the year," he says with a proud puff in his chest. "We'll finalize everything then."

Mom palms her chest and leans forward, eyes growing wide. "I can't wait. Six months of negotiations was a little much."

Dad laughs, like Mom is being dramatic. "My God, Helene, it wasn't *that* bad."

She turns to him, giving him a teasing yet incredulous simper. "It's all you talked about for one hundred and eighty dinners."

"Well, rest assured that topic of conversation will burden you no more." My father chuckles. "And don't forget, I'm whisking you away to Aspen next month for your troubles."

"Duly noted." Mom winks at him before placing her cake plate on the coffee table, and Dad reaches for her cappuccino mug and hands it over to her.

Almost forty years together, and they still have that special something, that glimmer in their eyes, an unspoken language, a bond no one else has ever been close to breaking.

I wonder if they know how lucky they are to have something so rare, but I don't have the energy to ask them. They'll see through it immediately, and I don't want to get their all-knowing stares and answer their prying questions.

My parents have a kingdom of luxury hotels to worry about—they don't need to worry about their only child on top of it all.

"Oh, Nic. I wanted to show you how the Gideon suite turned out in the SoHo reno." Dad pulls his phone from his pocket. "Helene, I left my glasses in the guest room on the nightstand. Would you mind?"

Mom smiles and slinks off without a word, and Dad leans in, placing his phone facedown on the coffee table.

I knew this was a setup.

"You doing okay, Nic?" he asks, his voice low and his forehead creased.

I jerk back, head angled. "What? Yes. Why?"

His mouth presses into a firm, straight line, and he breathes out of flared nostrils. "I got a call from our accountant the other day. He said there've been a few . . . sizable withdrawals from your trust in the last couple of months."

This is news to me.

I want to ask him how large these withdrawals are, but I don't want to give him any inkling that something isn't right.

The combination of cake and wine in my belly suddenly feels like a bad decision. The trust is in my name, but Brant has all my passwords, as well as access to my online account. He could've transferred shovelfuls of money to God knows where, and I wouldn't have noticed because I would have no reason to believe my husband would ever do such a thing. Not in this lifetime. Not in a million years.

I know he didn't have the best of role models growing up, but it never stopped him from being kind and generous, honest and forthright.

He always left my money alone—or so I thought.

They say the apple never falls far from the tree. It's a horrid, tired cliché, but I can't help but wonder if it applies in this case.

He might be Brant Gideon, but he's still a Gideon.

Mom returns with Dad's glasses in her hands, and he pulls his phone from the coffee table, picking up where he left off, which tells me Mom knows nothing about this and Dad is trying to protect my dignity because he believes something is amiss in my marriage.

If he only knew . . .

Gathering empty cake plates and silverware, I carry them to the kitchen without a word, thankful that my mother's return meant not having to finish this conversation with my father.

I rinse dishes in the sink a moment later, my hands trembling and eyes clouding with the burn of hot tears. As soon as my parents turn in for the night, I'll log in to my account and check into these withdrawals. As far as I'm aware, Brant hasn't made any new purchases. He hasn't rolled into the driveway in a flashy new car or gifted me with new diamonds.

Hell, even the suit he wore to the Bellhaus Museum the other week was two years old.

Nothing about any of this makes sense.

The only plausible explanation is that the money—*my* money—is buying his mistress's silence.

I scream.

But only in my head . . . where no one else can hear it.

CHAPTER 9

Wren

The dip of my bed and pull of my blanket stir me from a deep, winter sleep and a dream that I was quite enjoying because it was nothing like this cold, dark cabin. Mama was there. And Evie. It was warm, and we were playing ring-around-the-rosy outside.

But the more I come to, the more that dream disappears from my memory, and the more I'm aware of the fact that we are still alone.

Sage's body slides next to mine, followed by the repositioning of the layers of quilts, and then her arm wraps over my body, her fingertips icy. A small shiver runs through me until I get warm again . . . or at least, warm enough. I tuck the covers around us, running my hand along her shivering arm, but the lack of goose bumps tells me she isn't cold—she's scared.

Someone knocked on our door last night. We waited two hours before so much as looking out the window, and when we were sure the visitor had left, I ran to the henhouse—knife in hand—to retrieve the shotgun.

It was a sixty-foot sprint there and another sixty feet back, and while I didn't take time to check things out, it didn't seem like anything had been disturbed.

Perhaps we were imagining the knock? Perhaps it was the pop and crackle of the fire timed just so, or maybe an animal used our door as a scratching post?

It isn't long before the faint snores of my sister fill my left eardrum, and I find myself jealous of her once again.

As fatigued as I've been lately, I still struggle to fall asleep some nights, having to stare at the ceiling and count the ticks of the clock on the wall until I can't focus any longer. Some nights I've counted well past two thousand. Used to be I'd stay up and draw beside the fire on nights I couldn't sleep, but I wore my graphite pencils down to stubs, and we ran out of sketching paper shortly after Mama and Evie left.

Sometimes I want to draw so badly my fingers ache.

Those nights are pure torture.

Pulling in a frigid breath, I let it go and watch the clouds that form around me. Pitching myself up carefully, I rub my blurry eyes and try to focus on the dying fire in the hearth across the room.

Sage forgot to tend to the fire before bed.

Again.

Flinging the covers off us, I grab a couple of small logs and a poker and somehow, in my sleepy haze, manage to revive the fire.

Sliding my hands together, I place my palms toward the heat, and when I can no longer see my breath in the dark, I return to bed.

"I'm sorry, Wren," Sage whispers, eyes half-shut.

"It's okay. Go back to sleep."

I climb in beside her and press my body against hers, tucking my arm under hers. Sage's hair smells like Mama's milky lavender soap, and while I should find comfort in that, it only makes me miss her more.

Closing my eyes, I try again to fall asleep, only the moment I get comfortable, three knocks at the door fill our space.

I'd have almost thought I was having a bad dream if it weren't for Sage sitting up in bed, her eyes wide as saucers. She pulls the covers to her chin, trembling, and when she tries to say something, I clap my hand over her face, silencing her.

The knocks fill our cabin once more, this time harder, faster.

"I know someone's in there." The visitor's voice is deep, muffled by the wood that separates us, but I'm startled into action the second he pounds his fists against it a third time.

Springing out of bed, I make a run for the shotgun above the door. Positioning the step stool in front of the door, I climb up, balancing myself as I reach for the gun.

If this stranger—this intruder—dares to step foot inside our home, I won't hesitate to pull the trigger.

I have to protect Sage. Our home. Our belongings. Our life—or what's left of it.

My fingertips barely graze the metal barrel when the lock on the door gives and it swings open, knocking into me, and I lose my footing, toppling to the wooden floor, no gun in hand.

A gust of winter wind fills our home, and Sage screams.

There's a man in our house.

CHAPTER 10

Nicolette

I don't know what I'm looking for, but I'll know once I find it.

Brant's closet is meticulous for a creative type. There's order and organization and not a thing out of place. I'm sure he could locate his favorite cashmere sweater with his eyes closed, so I ensure that everything I touch or move goes back precisely the way I found it.

Scanning the shelves of folded jeans, the mirrored tray filled with his cologne staples—Botkier, Creed, and Burberry—and the drawer of neatly folded T-shirts and polos, I find nothing he hasn't worn a dozen times already.

Chewing the corner of my lip, I stand in the center of the small room, under an understated crystal chandelier that makes his closet feel more like the men's department at Barneys, and I release a defeated sigh.

He hasn't changed his cologne or purchased new clothes. He hasn't been working out any more than usual—opting to take his 5:00 AM runs and the occasional afternoon forest hike when he's feeling sluggish.

Every article I've read in the past few weeks is filled with tips and checklists and surefire ways to know whether or not your partner is cheating . . . and so far, Brant checks off none of those boxes.

Aside from the photo of the girl—which is still there, I've made sure of that—the only red flag I've come across is the transferring of thousands of dollars over the past several months. Each of the transactions—which range from a couple grand to five grand or more—appears to be going into a joint savings account that I believed we'd closed earlier this year. I remember signing the papers, and I remember him saying he'd run to town and stop by the bank to take care of the rest.

He lied . . .

From what I can gather, he's been making cash withdrawals from this savings account, and that's where the paper trail ends.

"What are you doing in here, Nic?"

Brant's voice echoes off the high ceiling and sends a quick tingle down my spine.

"Oh, my God," I say, turning to face him. "You scared me."

"Looking for something?" he asks, studying me. He must have shortened his morning run.

I've never been a good liar, which means I'm terrible at thinking on my feet.

"My Altuzarra belt," I say. "The black one with the gold buckle. I can't find it. Thought maybe it got placed in here with yours by mistake."

Brant's eyes search mine for an endless second, and then he strides away, moving across the hall to my half of our closet. When he returns, my black Altuzarra belt with the gold buckle is clenched in his fist.

He exhales through his nose. "This one?"

My mouth curls into a nonchalant smile. "Huh? I must have walked right by it."

I take the belt from him, steady my hand on his shoulder, and rise on my toes to kiss him, quietly breathing in his scent as if I might smell her on him. But alas, he smells like . . . Brant. Like the leather car seats of his Tesla and the alcohol wipes he cleans his camera lenses with and the remnants of Vetiver Body Wash from this morning's shower on his warm skin.

"I should start breakfast," I say, my hand resting on his chest for a moment as I pass him.

His breaths are harder than normal, and his gaze is unusually penetrative. I can only imagine what he's thinking. Either he's wondering what I'm looking for, or he's wondering why I'm looking for something in the first place.

Something tells me he knows the answer to both of those.

All these years together, I've never once snooped through any of his things.

I've never needed to.

Padding down the hall to the stairway, I bite my lip as I grip the banister and stop to digest what just happened.

I need to be more careful going forward . . . at least until I find my irrefutable evidence of whatever it is he's doing behind my back, it's important that I carry on like everything's fine. The second he suspects I'm onto him, he'll begin covering his tracks, and then I'll never find what I'm looking for.

Making my way to the kitchen, I preheat the oven and begin pulling out and arranging ingredients along the marble island. Midway between dicing the onions and peppers, I take a moment to tap the music app on my phone and stream some Fleetwood Mac through the kitchen speakers.

Like just another ordinary day . . .

But the second I pass the charging station, I spot Brant's phone plugged in to the wall. Glancing toward the bottom of the stairs, I ensure he's nowhere in sight before tapping the home button to wake the screen. That website with all the cheating-spouse tips had listed "changed phone passwords" as one of the top red flags, but I've yet to find Brant's phone without Brant nearby. The battery is low—almost dead. Was he on the phone for the last hour? The signal out here can be weak sometimes, depleting our batteries faster than usual if we talk on the phone too long.

A white notification box fills the glass, indicating there's an iMessage from a 212 number.

No preview.

No name attached to the contact.

Stealing a quick glance across the kitchen, I ensure once more that I'm completely alone before tapping in his password to unlock his device.

4 – 5 – 0 – 4

The anniversary of our first date.

The phone buzzes, prompting me to "try again."

4 – 5 – 0 – 4

Try again, it tells me again.

This is odd. The four-number password we've used for everything has always been 4504. The keypad to the garage. The pin code to our debit cards. The password on our security system.

My brows meet, and I look to the stairs again before trying another password.

8 – 9 – 7 – 9

His birth date.

The phone buzzes, asking me to try again.

I try my birth date.

Our wedding anniversary.

Our house number.

The last four of his Social Security number.

His phone vibrates, and the screen notifies me that the device has been locked for five minutes due to too many log-in attempts.

Shit.

Pulling in a deep breath, I return to the island and finish prepping vegetables. And as Stevie Nicks croons about the stillness of remembering what you lost and what you had, I whisper a silent prayer that my husband stays upstairs at least five more minutes . . .

CHAPTER 11

Wren

Sage shivers as I wrap my arms around her. We're hunched together on the edge of her bed in the corner of our cabin, covers wrapped around us as if they could possibly protect us from the strange monster who sits at our table and fusses with our kerosene lamp.

"Haven't used one of these in ages," he says as the flame begins to lick the inside of the glass.

The throw of light against his face highlight the marks and rivulets in his skin. Harsh lines and deep, scarred circles fill his cheeks and forehead and run from the corners of his nose to the sides of his mouth.

Mama told me once disease was rampant across our nation. She said people were always getting sick and dying, spreading horrible, incurable illnesses to one another.

I wonder if this man was sick once.

Or if he still is.

Shrugging out of his heavy jacket, he doesn't take his eyes off us once. "Feels good in here. Warm."

We don't speak, and I don't think Sage has blinked even once.

"Just you two out here?" he asks, crossing his legs and resting his booted ankle across his knee. He's a good-size man, and sitting in our small wooden chairs exaggerates his proportions.

Sage trembles, and I squeeze her tight.

"Seems awful strange to come across two young ladies, alone, in the middle of the woods," he says, slightly chuckling. "Sure no one else lives with you?"

I don't answer.

"You two got names?" he asks, peeling his hat off his head. His hair is dark and matted, like it hasn't been washed for a while, and he rakes his thick fingers through it, which only serves to make it worse. "How old are you?"

We continue in our silent standstill. He's a stranger. An intruder. We owe him nothing, and we don't have to answer his questions.

Leaning to the side, the man reaches to his back pocket, pulling something out and setting it on the table with a hard clunk. It's black and shiny with a barrel, like our rifle. It must be a smaller type of gun.

"You girls ever seen one of these?" He picks it up again, angling it toward us. The black metal shines in the light of the kerosene lamp.

My jaw clenches, sending an ache up the side of my face, and my palms dampen against Sage's nightdress. The prickle of sweat beneath my armpits follows next, and I realize I've yet to stop shaking since he barged in here and filled our home with his towering presence.

"Don't suppose you have any plug-ins out here?" he asks, glancing around our cabin. Rising, he makes his way around the room, his heavy boots clomping and shuffling against the wood floor. "You guys use electricity?"

I'm not sure what he's talking about. Whatever it is, I've never heard of it.

"You've got to be kidding me," the man says when he's done examining our kitchen setup. "This is some *Little House on the Prairie* shit."

I've read the books—the entire series is on our shelf in the corner—but I don't understand what he means or why it's so funny to him.

He collapses back into one of the kitchen chairs, and the spindles creak with his weight. I wish the stupid thing would just fall apart beneath him. If we could just disorient him for a moment, maybe we could run out of here. Then again, it's cold outside, and we wouldn't have time to properly lace our boots or secure our coats, and with no food or water or any idea of which direction to go, we'd likely die of hypothermia before the sun comes up.

"Where are your parents?" he asks, resting his shadowy jawline against his fist. From here, I see that his nails are caked in dirt, and I wonder how long he's been journeying through the forest. "I know it isn't just you two."

The stranger pinches the bridge of his nose.

"Look. I don't *want* to hurt you girls, but I'm looking for someone, and I feel like you could probably point me in the right direction, so if one of you doesn't speak up . . ." He rises, his towering height blocking the warmth and glow of light from the fireplace. Tromping across the room, he makes his way to Sage's bed and, without saying another word, reaches out toward us.

I shut my eyes and hold on to my sister so tight she yelps, but in an instant, I lose her, her skin sliding beneath my grip as he jerks her out of my arms.

"Wren!" my sister cries, and I peer through one squinted eye.

He has her now.

All that's left beside me is a cold void and a mess of blankets.

Her nails dig into his arms, but he doesn't so much as flinch.

Wearing a leer that turns my blood to ice, he stares at me with squinted eyes. "Let's try this again. *What's your name?*"

My chest squeezes when I notice the thick tears gliding down my sister's pale cheeks.

If he does anything to her, it'll be my fault.

I didn't hold on tight enough.

I stubbornly refuse to answer him, but finally I say, "Wren."

"And hers?" His arm rests beneath her pointed chin, covering her entire neck. One powerful squeeze would snap the life right out of her small body.

"Sage," I say, eyes darting from hers to his and back.

"How old are you?" he asks.

"Nineteen," I answer, swallowing the lump in my throat. "She's eighteen."

"Where are your parents?"

"Our mother went to town to get supplies," I lie. "She'll be back soon—any minute now."

His lips pull up at the side, revealing sallow teeth, but this isn't a happy smile.

"You think I'm an idiot?" He squeezes my sister tighter, and she gulps for air. "I've been coming around here for days. Nobody here but you two." The man glances around. "But I see over there, you've got four beds. And on the wall, I see four hooks, but I only see two coats. Lie to me again, *Wren*, and you're not going to like what happens."

I have to look away.

"So who else is missing from the party?" he asks.

I'm afraid to lie to him, so I blurt out the truth. "Our sister, Evie. She went with Mama to town."

His hold on Sage appears to loosen, but he isn't letting her go just yet. His uneven brows rise, and he rubs his lips together, like he's thinking hard about something.

"Your mother is Maggie Sharp," he says. "Isn't she?"

Shaking my head, I say, "I don't know who that is."

I've never once thought about whether Mama had a proper name or not. I called her Mama, Sage called her Mama, and so did Evie. There was never a reason to call her anything else.

"Bullshit," he says, spittle flying off his lips. "What's your mama's name then?"

"She doesn't have one." My voice shakes. I speak the truth, but the way he looks at me makes me feel like I'm fibbing.

His barrel of a chest rises and falls as his head cocks to one side. "Don't play games with me, Wren."

Placing my hand across my galloping heart, I say, "Honest. She's just . . . Mama."

"What'd your daddy call her?" he asks.

"I don't know. I don't remember."

"How can you not remember?"

"He died a long time ago," I say. Along with our older sister, Imogen, but I don't share that with the stranger because it's neither here nor there. "We were young. I don't remember him much, so I don't remember what he called Mama."

I don't even know his name . . . just that the number of times Mama spoke about him and Imogen I could count on one hand. It made her sad, talking about the past and how things used to be. I can't imagine losing your husband and your first child would be something you'd want to bring up more than you had to. Seeing her blue eyes turn glassy as she struggled to keep her composure always tore me up, so after a while, I stopped asking.

Their bodies are buried out back, their graves marked by a weeping willow tree and a bed of red impatiens that Mama plants every spring because they were Imogen's favorites.

All I really know about them is that Daddy had auburn hair and a big laugh and Imogen looked just like me.

"You could've been twins," Mama always told me. *"Spitting image of your big sister."*

The stranger groans, rising and letting Sage go. She falls to the floor, then scrambles across the room and back into my arms.

"I've been walking these woods for days," he says. "I'm tired, and I don't have much patience left. Now, I don't want to snap on you girls or do something I'll regret in the morning, so I'm going to let you get to bed, and we'll try this again when the sun comes up."

Sage glances up at me, and I try to steady my breath so I can calm down.

He dims the kerosene light until the flame dies down and then shoves his gun into the waist of his pants before ambling across the cabin toward Mama's bed. Wrapping his meaty hands around the footboard, he begins to shove his body weight against it. The wood spindles screech against the floor as the bed slides forward, and he grunts with each push.

I don't ask what he's doing.

I already know.

By the time he's finished, the bed is pushed up against the door—our only way out save for a couple of small windows. As soon as the bed is positioned where he wants it, the man kicks off his boots and unbuttons his flannel shirt. A moment later, he's under one of Mama's quilts, wasting no time getting cozied up.

"Go to sleep now, girls," he says. "Morning'll be here soon."

Slipping my hand into my sister's, I lead her to Evie's bed, the one farthest from this stranger, and we climb in. I let her go first, hoping she'll feel safer if she's sleeping between the wall and myself, and I tuck the covers around us.

Turning on my side, I keep a squinted eye on the man, because my gut tells me not to let him out of my sight for more than a second.

I'll watch him all night long if it means keeping us safe.

And alive.

Besides, I couldn't sleep if I tried.

Not with him here.

Not when I don't know who he is or what he wants with us.

Or what he's planning to do to us tomorrow.

CHAPTER 12

Nicolette

"When does your flight leave?" My husband runs his fingertip along a row of book spines at the bookshop on Hancock Drive—Stillwater Hills' gentrified version of Main Street, where every shop and storefront has been fashioned from an old Victorian or Tudor-style manse leftover from Stillwater's coal mining heyday.

This is what we do on Saturdays. We grab brunch at a sleepy café by the side of the road where they know us by name, and then we head to Raven Books to pick up the latest bestsellers before returning home for an afternoon of going our own ways—which for Brant means holing up in his office and for me means laundry, cleaning, and phone calls with friends and family. Sometimes I'll take a bubble bath if I'm bored. Maybe do some online shopping from some of my favorite NYC boutiques that knew me by name a lifetime ago.

It never used to be this way, though.

Our Saturdays used to be spent between the sheets, peppered with breaks for things like showering and wine refills. We called them Naked Saturdays, which was beyond cheesy at the time, but now that they're gone, I can't remember when I stopped missing them or when he stopped wanting them, and that says something.

"Didn't I tell you?" I ask. Brant turns to me, one sandy-blond brow lifted. "I'm not going this year."

His hand falls from the spine of *The Alchemist*, and he angles his body toward me. "Not going? As in, not going at all?"

I understand where he's coming from. For the entirety of our marriage, I've spent the coldest months in Miami with my best friend, Cate. The sunshine and extra vitamin D has always helped stave off the winter blues, plus Cate is a riot. My friendship with her is one that I'll cherish always, and while I could use a good distraction right now, I can't go.

Not with all these unanswered questions lingering.

"Nic . . ." Brant's voice softens, and I know he's going to try to reason with me. "You sure about this?"

I nod, turning my attention to the book selection before me. Plucking a copy of *Atlas Shrugged* from the shelf, I begin to page through it as I've done a thousand times before, hoping this time it might capture my interest the way these kinds of books have always captured Brant's, but alas, my tastes are still as commercial as ever.

"But," he says, coming close, "you know how you get this time of year . . ."

Flipping the pages, I sigh. "I do."

"And your bad dreams," he says, as if I need reminding, as if I could possibly forget the reoccurring dreams about the empty, abandoned baby stroller that always seem to plague me in the colder months. They're not pleasant by any means, but I'm used to them now. I've chalked them up as a metaphor that represents my inability to have a child, and the winter months with their barren trees and quiet skies serve as my yearly reminder.

"I'm not going to let my nightmares dictate whether or not I go to Florida."

"How does Cate feel about this?" he asks.

"She was disappointed of course, but she was supportive. Says she'll come up here and spend a few weeks with me if I want," I say. And it's true. She could sense in my voice that something wasn't right, but I couldn't tell her then. This is the kind of thing you don't gab about with your best friend over the phone. These are the things you talk about in person—and only when you have enough proof that you don't seem like a bored and lonely housewife manufacturing drama because you're feeling insecure.

"Maybe you could still go, but for only a few weeks?" he suggests. "A month. Tops."

I smirk, trying to brush him off as casually as possible. "You worry too much."

"I guess . . . I guess I just don't understand," he says. The fact that he won't let this go is concerning, but it isn't a surprise. If anything, it simply confirms what I already thought—he wants me to go.

Maybe even *needs* me to go.

Turning to Brant, I say with a smile, "Is there something wrong with wanting to spend more time with my husband?"

"Of course not. I'm just worried your . . . *blues* . . . will come back with a vengeance."

There was that one winter—the year I had the hysterectomy after a bout of profuse bleeding that left me lying unconscious on the floor. Brant rushed me to the local ER. Everything else happened so quickly, almost as if in a vacuum of bad memories better forgotten.

I vaguely recall spending 80 percent of my day sleeping during my recovery, wasting away to bones and using what little energy I had left listening to Brant talking to my doctor on the phone in the next room over. He was worried about me then, worried I wouldn't bounce back and be the girl he married, worried I'd never laugh or smile again. He kept using the word "traumatic," but I think there are worse things people could go through.

At least I'm still alive.

But the thing that sticks out the most to me about that time in my life is that Brant easily could have left me back then, he could have handed me back to my parents and washed his hands of me—but he didn't.

He stayed.

And he took care of me.

He loved me through it all. Through the crying fits and the empty stroller dreams, through the mood swings and lethargy.

"It's been a long time since that happened," I remind him. That first winter was brutal, and I'm still not convinced it wasn't triggered by a hormonal imbalance from the procedure, but I'm not the one with the Harvard medical diploma hanging on my wall, so my suggestions were always shot down.

"Right. Because you always go to Cate's for the winter." He hasn't turned away from me since the moment this conversation started, and now he's resting a hand on his hip. His frustration is an inch thick and building. "Are you sure this is what you want to do?"

Glancing back at him, I ask with a chuckle, "Why? Is this going to mess up your winter plans or something?"

"Nic." His expression falls, and he doesn't laugh. Apparently he doesn't appreciate that I'm not taking his concerns seriously. "I'm trying to have an earnest discussion here, and this is an issue that's extremely important to me."

My stomach sinks, and I'm convinced this is double-talk. His concern isn't me so much as it is preventing me from finding out about whatever it is he's hiding.

"Please don't make this into a thing," I say. "I've given this a lot of thought. I've been on antidepressants for a decade now, and I want to see if I can make it through a winter up here. If it gets too hard, I promise you can put me on the next plane to Miami, and I won't put up a fight. Just . . . let me see if I can do this. I'd at least like to try."

His green eyes soften, and he reaches for my hand, lifting it to deposit a kiss. "I love you so much, Nic. I'm sorry. I just . . . I worry."

"Too much," I say, head tilted and lips curled so he thinks I find this more endearing than unnerving.

"Too much," he echoes, pressing his lips against my fingers before giving me a soundless kiss. "I just want you to be happy. And I don't know what I'd do if anything happened to you."

CHAPTER 13

Wren

Sage stirs at the sound of the stranger shuffling around our cabin just as the sun peeks through the curtains above the kitchen sink.

I haven't slept.

Wrapping my arm around her to keep her from startling, I watch as the man rummages through our cupboards, tossing measuring cups to the floor and shoving dishes aside.

"We don't have much food," I say, sitting up, "if that's what you're looking for."

He chuffs. "You have to have something. Can't imagine you're living off water and air."

The man turns away from me and glances through the kitchen window toward our goat corral. I can't let him kill them. They're not for meat—they're for milk, which we use for cooking, baking, and making the artisanal cheeses and butters and soaps Mama would have the supply man sell at the market every few months, all of them tied with colored twine and blessed with a prayer.

The goats are our livelihood.

We can't afford to lose a single one.

"We have some potatoes in the root cellar," I say, sliding out of bed.

After I make my way across the room, I begin to step into my boots when I sense his presence over me in the form of a shadow.

"Wait," he says.

I say nothing, averting my eyes. Looking into his beady squint makes the burning bile in my stomach rise into my throat.

He offers a slight chuckle, his hands resting on his hips. "You girls don't need to be so scared of me."

Said the wolf to the lamb . . .

"You two haven't stopped shaking since I got here. Makes me think you're going to try to do something stupid if I let you out of here," he says. "I didn't come here to hurt you."

"Then why are you here?" I force myself to look at him, and my stiff muscles quake.

"Right now I want some damn breakfast," he says, shuffling away. "Long as you come right back, I'll let you go to the henhouse."

It's then that I remember there are only two hens left, which means there'll only be two eggs for the day. I'm sure the stranger will eat them both.

"Go." He points at me. "And I want you back in two minutes."

He looks to my sister, then back at me—a threat perhaps? And a second later, he moves Mama's bed away from the door.

I throw on my jacket and lace my boots before grabbing the basket by the door and braving the cold. Unforgiving wind whips my hair across my face as I trudge across the sod. Once inside, I find the two Leghorns still clucking, and I locate two warm eggs to take back.

Stopping at the root cellar on my way back, I grab three small potatoes and some goat's-milk butter for frying.

As soon as I'm back in the cabin, I find the man washing up over our basin, helping himself to Mama's pink toothbrush and sullying our clean water with the filth from his hands and face. I'll have to make a trip to the well later this morning—that is, if he lets me.

Placing the basket of eggs on the kitchen counter alongside the potatoes and butter, I pull a dull paring knife from one of the drawers and begin chopping, each slice requiring brute strength to cut through the earthy flesh. A second later, Sage is at my side, making herself useful. I imagine she wants to stick close to me more than she cares about cooking for this man.

In tense silence, we get busy fixing breakfast, and from the corner of my eye, I spot the man shrugging out of his shirt and rinsing it in the basin we use to wash our faces and brush our teeth. He uses our soap to scrub it clean before wringing out the water, and then he hangs it on a hook near the fireplace. All that covers his broad shoulders and veiny muscles now is a shirt missing fabric where the sleeves should be.

Everything about him is strange and unpredictable. He's just as wild as anything that lurks beyond the pines.

Returning to the kitchen table, he watches us prepare the meal, his stare heavy and unwelcome. When I finally plate his food and bring it to him, he peers up at me and then down at the food.

"You girls going to eat?" he asks, yanking the fork from my hand and pulling his dish closer. "Or you just going to stand there and stare? Didn't your mama teach you that staring is rude?"

He chuckles, huffing through his hooked nose.

Sage tucks her head and folds her arms around her small waist, and I glance back toward the pan with a few potatoes left in it.

We gave him both of the eggs.

We were afraid not to.

Without saying a word, my sister and I divide the remaining food and take the seats across from him. My unsettled stomach rolls when I take my first bite, hunger mixing with nerves, but I force myself to chew and swallow, repeating a few more times until my plate is empty.

Sage pushes her potatoes around, and I nudge her under the table. The food might be cold and her appetite may be gone, but she needs to eat . . . especially if we want a chance at getting out of here.

I had lain awake all night dreaming up an escape. *He's going to notice if we pack bags. He's going to notice if we leave to gather eggs and don't return after a short bit. A few minutes isn't near enough of a head start anyway. Plus, I don't think he'd let us both leave the house together at the same time. Besides, once we get past the tree line, I don't have the slightest clue which direction to run, and there's a chance we could get lost in the forest, or worse: become some hungry animal's dinner.*

The thought of getting away from him is equally as terrifying as staying.

The man finishes his breakfast, wiping his greasy mouth on the back of his hair-covered arm. Leaning to the side, he retrieves a green and white rectangular box from his pocket, along with a little blue tube with a red button on the end.

Tapping the box on the table, a long white stick pokes out, and he takes it between his lips. Next, he drags his thumb along one side of the little tube and presses the red button. In an instant, a tiny flame appears.

Sage and I watch as he brings the miniature fire to the stick and sucks in, his chest rising. The tip burns, glowing red, then orange, until wisps of gray smoke rise, filling the air with a distinct, ashy scent much different from the one coming from our hearth.

Drawing in a long breath, he pinches the stick between his thumb and forefinger before releasing a cloud of white that obscures his face for a few seconds.

My sister coughs.

I hold my breath.

I don't like the way it smells: unfamiliar, aggressive, displeasing—like him.

"You girls know it's Christmas, right?" he asks, his dark-blue gaze moving between us.

I nod. I hadn't planned on celebrating this year, so I didn't bring it up to Sage. Didn't seem right to exchange gifts without Mama and

Evie here. And besides, it's not like we have anything here for a proper Christmas feast.

"Must be hard being away from your mama today." He brings the white stick to his lips again, exhaling more smoke a second later. "Where do you think she is?"

I reach for Sage's hand under the table, giving it a squeeze and hoping she interprets it as me telling her to keep her yap shut.

"Awfully strange to me that a mother would abandon her daughters on Christmas," he says. "Something about that just seems . . . off to me."

He studies us, sucking on the stick until the end glows cherry red and a pile of ash lands on the table, which he brushes onto the floor.

"She'll be back," I say. "Wouldn't be surprised if she walked in that door today."

The stick dangles from the corner of his mouth, as if it could fall at any moment. "You're a terrible liar."

My eyes flick to his.

"Tell me, Wren," he says, taking another puff. "What's your mama look like?"

This stranger's fascination with a woman he's never met before makes the hair on the back of my neck rise.

Clearing my throat and licking my lips, I sit up straight. Half of me wants to lie. The other half of me is scared of what he'd do to us if I did.

"Blonde hair," I say. "But dark blonde. Dark-blue eyes. Gray almost. And she's tall—taller than me."

I hold my hand several inches above the top of my head, remembering how we always measured our height according to Mama's. I stopped growing when I finally reached her chin.

The man stubs his white stick into the wooden top of our table, leaving a black mark on the wood, and then he flicks it into the fireplace. Leaning back in the chair, he folds his arms across his chest as he examines me.

"That could be anyone," he says. "You got a pic?"

"A what?"

"A picture," he says. "A photograph."

My brows furrow. "No."

"You ever had your picture taken?" he asks. "With a camera?"

He holds his hands up in front of his face, fingers curled, though I'm not sure what he's miming.

"No," I say.

"Well, shit." He drags his palm along his bristled face, and the sound it makes sends a prickled crawl up my skin. "Who does she look like more? You or your sister?"

I glance toward Sage, who's never looked much like Mama to begin with. They don't share a single feature. Mama always said Sage favored Daddy with her fine features and lily-white complexion, but no one knows where the dark hair came from.

"Me," I say, though Mama doesn't look much like me either.

One day we stood side by side in front of the mirror, cleaning up for the night, and I compared our features. Mama'd given us a biology lesson earlier that day, told us about genetics and Punnett squares, so naturally I was curious, but it didn't take more than a few minutes for me to realize she and I didn't share a single trait. Mama's nose was distinct, slightly large for her face, and her lashes were shorter than mine. My eyes were hooded, hers more defined. My face was round, hers long. Her brows were darker and fuller than mine, and she had a dimple in the center of her left cheek when she smiled. Her hair was a dark blonde—creek-water blonde, Mama called it—and mine matched the August sunshine, soft and golden.

When I asked Mama why we looked so different, she laughed, ruffled my hair, and told me that genetics were a funny thing and that sometimes we might look more like our grandparents or aunts or cousins than our mama or daddy, and then she proceeded to tell me how much I reminded her of her own mother, right down to the starbursts of white in my blue irises.

"Her mouth is shaped like a heart," I say, my chest tightening when I think about how much I miss her smile. "Her upper lip . . ." I trace the shape in the air with my fingertip. "It's like this."

"A cupid's bow," he says.

I'm not sure what he means by a cupid's bow, but I don't care to tell him that.

I take a moment to gather myself, pulling in a ragged breath as he waits for me to continue, but there's nothing more to say. Mama's face is burned in my memory for always, but no amount of describing her to a stranger could ever convey how beautiful she is.

She always reminded me of a storybook queen—the noble kind—with love in her heart that translated through the softness in her tone when she spoke to us and the sparkle of contentedness in her eyes when she'd wrap us in her arms and read to us before bed each night.

Squeezing my eyes, I try to force away the damp burn so he doesn't see me cry.

"Does she have a mark right here?" The stranger points to a spot on the right side of his nose. "A bump. The color of her skin. Hard to see unless you were in the right light."

My heart stops beating for a single, endless second.

"No," I lie. "She doesn't."

CHAPTER 14

Nicolette

Brant zips his suitcase closed before taking a seat beside me on our bed. Cupping my cheek, he runs the pad of his thumb along my bottom lip before stealing a kiss.

If it were last year, I'd be in Florida by now, soaking in the sunshine, my toes buried in sugar-white sand as the sea spray and humidity flatten and frizz my hair and Cate tells me some salacious story about her dating life.

I've always lived for my time with her. Winters in upstate New York are cloudy and bleak. Winters with Cate are carefree, hilarious, and Technicolor. Her home is right on the water, and nothing compares to waking up to the sound of the Atlantic crashing on the shore or the caws of seagulls as they hover over the coastline.

For years, I'd hinted to Brant about wanting to live somewhere warm and green and lush, but he wouldn't have it. He said, "Until we're white-haired and retired, we have no business subjecting ourselves to a Floridian lifestyle. We'll get fat and lazy and spoiled by the sunshine." Plus, he likes being close to New York, saying he can be on a plane in a matter of hours and fly anywhere in the world at a moment's notice should he be needed.

So I settled for winters with Cate.

Artists are strange, fickle souls. His creativity exhausts him some moments; other times it lights a fire so bright inside of him, I can almost see the flares in his eyes. He comes alive then, all of him, all at once. It's beautiful and contagious and part of the reason I fell in love with him in the first place.

But lately, he's been feeling stifled and blocked—or so he says. He's been doubting himself and pressuring himself, feeling like an unworthy impostor one minute and a washed-up has-been the next—Bellhaus Museum exhibit or not.

My husband takes my hands in his. "You sure you'll be okay here?"

"I offered to join you."

We already had this conversation, after I told him I was staying in New York for the winter. I offered to accompany him on this trip, intentionally waiting until his connecting flight from Dallas to the Mariscal Sucre International Airport was full.

I agreed with him that it didn't make sense for me to join him on this trip, but what I didn't agree with was the relief in his eyes when he realized we were on the same page.

"I'll check on you every day," he says. "And I'll have my phone on me the whole time."

Is he overcompensating? Reminding me that he's available by phone, night or day, because he feels guilty about whatever it is he's hiding?

"I'll be fine." I rise from the bed, sliding my hands in the back pockets of my jeans and mustering a smile.

Brant slides his bag off the bed and wheels it to the doorway of our master suite before checking his phone—the same one he inexplicably locked me out of this week—and then he puts it away.

"My ride's two minutes away," he says. Our eyes catch. There's worry in his squint and in the hard lines on his forehead—I just can't distinguish if it's for me or for himself.

I follow him to the landing at the bottom of the stairs, and he props his bag by the door before turning to me.

"I'm going to miss you," he says, brushing a strand of hair from my forehead.

"Me too." I say it back but only because I need to keep up appearances.

Brant angles my mouth toward his, his fingers gently pushing the underside of my chin, and then he kisses me again, harder and greedier than usual.

His phone dings in his pocket, and from my peripheral vision, I spot a black sedan pulling into the driveway.

"Your ride's here," I say, backing away.

Brant massages his lips together, surveying me for a moment, but I pat his chest with the palm of my hand and step aside.

"Be safe," I tell him, as I always do. My husband twists the knob on the front door, and I kiss the pads of my fingertips before giving him a wave.

"Oh, Brant?" I ask.

"Yes?" He turns back to me.

"Forgot to tell you . . . there was a fraud alert on my trust account," I say, brows meeting. I specifically waited until this moment, until he'd be on his way out of the country so he wouldn't have a chance to cover his tracks. "I told them just to freeze it until we can figure out what's going on."

"Hm." His Adam's apple bobs, and his tan complexion whitens for a hair of a second. "That's . . . concerning. I'll look into it when I get back. I'm sure it's nothing."

He lingers in the doorway but only for a moment, and then he's gone.

CHAPTER 15

Wren

"Eat up, girls," the stranger says, peeling a strip of goat's meat from a rib. "Waste not, want not."

Mama always says that.

The overpowering scent of the charred meat on my plate fills my nostrils. I've yet to take a bite, but I already know all the spices in the cupboard aren't going to make us forget what we're about to eat is one of our favorite goats.

Sage threw up when we were preparing the food earlier.

She looked outside at the blood and pelt lying in the brown grass, where he'd shot one of them earlier today, and it got to her. She loved those goats the way we all loved the little collie dog we once had before he ran away.

I begged the man not to kill the goats this morning, but he grabbed our shotgun and marched outside, slamming the door behind him.

The sound of the blast rang through the cabin, clattering the windows, and my sister and I held each other until he came back in a blood-spattered jacket to dig a hunting knife from his bag.

"I'll be damned if I eat eggs and potatoes for every damn meal," he'd said with a huff.

Picking at the meat on my plate, I tear off a chunk. The warm, heady scent fills my nostrils, and I slide the piece into my mouth. The taste is stronger than chicken, and the texture is firm, chewy almost.

Elbowing Sage, I whisper, "Eat."

If the poor goat is already dead, we might as well eat it. It'd be a shame if it died for the sole purpose of feeding the stranger.

I'm still not sure what he's doing here—all I've gathered at this point is that he knows who Mama is . . . but he won't tell us how or why he's looking for her.

"You two always lived here?" he asks, picking a piece of meat from between his teeth and making a sucking noise.

"Yes," I say, though I neglect to tell him that I've had these memories fill my head sometimes, memories of living in a house with flowered paper on the walls and fuzzy soft floors that tickled my feet when I ran across them.

Mama said it was probably a "false memory," maybe something I picked up from one of those books I always kept my nose in.

I could never understand; if those memories were false, then why'd they feel so real?

"So let me get this straight," he says, sitting up and pointing his fork at us. "You've lived here, in this cabin, your entire lives?"

I nod.

"You ever go to school?" he asks. "With other kids? To learn?"

We look at each other before shaking our heads. Mama said schools weren't safe anymore, that there were parents who sent their kids off to school in the morning, never to see them again.

"We had lessons," I say.

"Lessons?" he asks.

"Reading, writing, addition, and subtraction," I say. "Sometimes history or geography."

History always made Mama sad, though, and I realized once that she was giving us a condensed version of events when I was paging through one of her books on social injustices and stumbled across an entry for a man by the name of Martin Luther King Jr.; I read about his fight for peace and equality and how he was killed for it.

I knew then that Mama left certain things out for a reason.

She only wanted to protect us, to shield us from all the ways the world had gone mad.

"Ever seen a TV?" he asks. The man shakes his head and huffs. "Of course not. You don't even have electricity."

"What's a . . . *tee* . . . *vee*?" Sage asks.

"Television," he says. "You can watch shows. Movies."

The words don't register with Sage, but I remember Mama once talking about having something like that when she was a kid. Said she'd come home after school and watch her favorite shows until her parents came home from work and changed it to the news. The news always depressed her because it was nothing but people talking about all the bad things going on in the world. She never understood why her parents wanted to watch it.

The only thing Mama liked about TV was watching the weather forecast. She grew up in a place called La Jolla; it was in southern California, where it was always sunny and warm and she could play outside every single day. Then her daddy took a job in New York state. She was never able to go back to La Jolla. Too expensive, she said. But she promised to take us there . . . someday.

"There's a screen," he says, tracing the shape of a rectangle in the air with his fingertips. "And there are people on it, acting out . . . things . . . I don't know how to describe it. It's for entertainment. When you're bored."

I return to the lukewarm meat on my plate, pushing it around with my fork and preparing myself to take another bite.

"You two are missing out, I'm telling you," he says, shoveling a forkful into his mouth. "You're going to be in for a real treat once I get you out of this primitive hell."

My fork falls, clinking against my tin plate. "What do you mean . . . get us out?"

The man narrows his gaze. "I'm leaving in a few days. You two are coming with me."

"We're not allowed to leave," Sage says before I get a chance to respond.

The stranger shrugs. "Says who? Your mama? Your mama who isn't here right now? Your mama who left you to die out here all by yourselves?"

I tighten my jaw as my fist coils around my fork to keep me from up and stabbing his hand with the dull tines.

"She didn't leave us here to die," I say.

He lifts a brow, head cocked, and then he snickers. "Yeah, well, it looks that way to me. Don't know any mother who would leave her young daughters all alone in the woods without enough food to get through winter."

"I'd rather starve to death here than go anywhere with you," I say. "If you want to kill us, just leave us here."

I've done the math with our supplies. We'll likely be dead by the end of next month.

The stranger lets out a bellow of a laugh that almost makes him look nice. "*Kill* you? What makes you think I want to *kill* you?"

"Then what do you want?" I ask.

His shoulders square with mine as he situates in his chair. "It's complicated. But you'll know soon enough."

"Evie's sick," Sage says out of nowhere, though maybe she's just trying to change the subject to something she can understand. "Mama took Evie to town to get help. She needed medicine. They'll come back once Evie's well."

When she says it out loud like that, it makes me realize for the first time just how ridiculous it sounds to keep faith that they're still coming back.

My last thread of hope vanishes in that moment.

The stranger covers his smirk with the dirty palm of his hand, laughing at her naivety.

"Hate to break it to you," he says, reaching his fork across the table and stealing our uneaten meat, "but she's not coming back."

Sage turns to me, her dark eyes brimming, and I slip my hand into hers, threading our fingers together.

He finishes his cooked goat and pushes his plate toward us. "Been a long day, girls. Think I'm going to catch a nap."

Rising from the table, he heads to Mama's bed, wrapping his greasy hands around the spindles and shoving it in front of the door again. A second later, he plucks his hat off one of the bedposts and nestles himself beneath the covers, his face hidden.

Without making too much noise, we clear the table and pump the sink with water to wash dishes.

"Wren," Sage whispers, leaning toward me, "why do you think he's looking for Mama?"

Squinting at her, I lift my finger to my lips and silently shush her. That man is maybe twenty feet across the room from us, and he isn't yet snoring. We can't risk him hearing us talk about *anything*.

Eyeing the chalkboard calendar in the corner, above the bookshelves where Mama would gather us on a braided rug for our lessons, I spot our slate boards and a tin can of white chalk.

Tiptoeing across the room, I grab two slates and two chalks and begin to write my first message to Sage. The chalk squeaks as I drag it across the board, and I stop, my heart in my teeth. We both glance toward the man, but he doesn't so much as stir.

Pressing softer this time, I write out: WE CAN'T LET HIM HEAR US TALK.

Sage nods, writing a message on her board: I'M SCARED.

"I know," I mouth, writing another message: I'M GOING TO GET US OUT OF HERE.

HOW? She writes.

Lifting my shoulders to my ears, I mouth, "I don't know." And then I write another message: I'LL FIGURE IT OUT TONIGHT. Erasing that message, I write another: WE'RE GOING TO HAVE TO LEAVE LIKE MAMA AND EVIE.

Sage's dark eyes widen, and she chews the inside corner of her lower lip, a little indentation on the side of her neck pulsing.

Writing one last message before we finish the dishes, I hold it up for her to see: I WON'T LET ANYTHING HAPPEN TO US.

CHAPTER 16

NICOLETTE

The fireplace crackles and a strong cup of coffee rests on a marble coaster to my right as I click through Brant's social media and email accounts. Miraculously enough, he hasn't changed any of those passwords—they're still "BGNG777."

Brant should've landed in Ecuador by now, completely unaware of what I'm doing thousands of miles away, across oceans and continents. I can't help but feel dirty for snooping through his accounts, but after everything I've stumbled across lately, what choice do I have?

His inbox is clean.

Typical Brant.

A few junk emails from the day filter in, but nothing unusual. I click through his sent folder next, finding nothing but boring correspondence between himself and potential buyers. Clicking through his folders, I start with the one marked "Important" followed by the one marked "Nic," which seems to hold nothing more than email confirmations related to gift purchases he's made for me in recent years.

Of course he hasn't changed his email password—there's nothing remotely damning in here.

Navigating to his Facebook account, I go through his messages, most of them from female fans. Some going so far as to include propositions and topless photos. Each message has been read, but he's never replied to a single one, from what I can tell.

I wonder what that means . . . that he's never mentioned these messages to me before. Was he trying to protect me from them? Or was he trying to ensure I had no reason to doubt his loyalty to me?

For a solid hour, I pore over every hidden pocket of his social media accounts, only to come up empty-handed. From a private browsing window on my phone, a quick visit to a forum called cheaterfinder.net suggests I comb through our cell phone account as well. Minutes later, I'm perusing every cell phone e-statement I can get my hands on, scanning each and every number that has called Brant's phone over the past several months.

Of the numbers I can't recognize, only one of them shows up repeatedly. It's a 212 number, and this New York caller only seems to ring him on Friday mornings, between nine and ten—when I'm in town doing the weekly shopping.

As I sink back into the sofa cushions, my blood alternates between hot and cold, as if my entire being can't decide which way to feel in this moment, so it feels everything all at once.

A moment later, I perform a quick Google search of this number, but it yields no usable results. Logging in to my trust account next, I check the dates on the withdrawals. My mouth runs dry when I realize they correspond with the phone calls.

What are you doing, Brant?

CHAPTER 17

Wren

"Aren't you too old to play with dolls?" the stranger asks Sage that night after supper. His stale breath fills the air around us when he talks, and even from across the room, his sharp, musty odor invades our space.

He gave himself a sponge bath earlier, using one of Evie's lace-trimmed washcloths and forcing us to stand with our faces to the wall as he undressed. Being in the same room as a naked man for the first time sent a hot flush to my cheeks, but I was grateful because if he didn't want me to see him, it meant he probably wasn't going to make me touch him.

I know what men do with women. I read about it in a book once. Mama said it was trash, and she didn't know how that book got mixed in with the others. That night she burned it in the fire, but I couldn't stop thinking about what that fictional couple did. The way he kissed her. The way she touched him. Even now, my heart ricochets just thinking about it.

But the thought of the stranger doing any of those things to me forces a hint of bile up the back of my throat, and I have to look away.

"What's it to you?" I ask him now.

His thick brows lift, as if my mettle surprises him, and he says, "Just never seen a young lady your age play with dolls, that's all."

"They make her happy," I say. "Let her be."

He places his palms in the air, a silent protest perhaps, and then he pulls a shiny, rectangular item out of his bag. It's completely black on all sides and smooth as glass, almost otherworldly.

Next he digs into his bag and pulls out a long white string, only it's thicker than the kind of string we sew with, and he sticks one end of it into the black rectangle and the other end into a silver square.

"Gotta get this charged up before we leave tomorrow," he says.

"What is that?" Sage asks, rocking in her chair by the fire.

He holds it up. "It's called a cell phone. You use it to call people. Everyone's got one of these . . . everyone but you guys." Lifting the silver square, he adds, "And this is a power bank. It's how I have to charge this thing since you guys live like it's 1881."

The stranger laughs, his chest rising and falling a couple of times, and then he pushes his cell phone aside.

I found something like that once, in the wooden box Mama keeps under her bed. I was looking for an extra spool of yellow thread to hem Evie's dress, but before I had time to examine the strange black rectangle, I heard Mama's voice outside the window.

The next time she stepped outside and I found myself alone inside the cabin, I tried to steal another look at it, but by then it was gone. I never asked Mama about it after that. I didn't want to get in trouble for being nosy.

Glancing toward his bag, I can't help but wonder what other things he has in there. From what I've been able to gather, he'd been trekking through the forest for at least a few days before he found us, so whatever's in that bag were things he needed to survive out there.

I managed to get a few hours of sleep last night, but only because my body took over my mind long enough to let it happen, but in the still, quiet hours, lying in the pitch-blackness of the cabin while the man snored and Sage's breath was warm against the back of my neck, it occurred to me that getting out of here might not be as difficult as I thought it was going to be . . .

Everything we need has been in front of us this entire time.

Behind the mirror above the basin is Mama's medicine cabinet, where she stores rubbing alcohol and cotton swabs, bandages and salves, aloe vera and camphor and aspirin, but most importantly melatonin and valerian root—sleep aids.

Tomorrow night when Sage and I prepare supper, I'm going to crush the tablets and mix them into his food. I'll triple, quadruple the doses if I have to—anything to put him out so we can set off as soon as the sun goes down.

If we leave on foot under a dark sky, it'll be harder for him to track us, and if he does wake and realize we're gone, he'll be so disoriented from the herbs, it'll only make things worse for him if he does go after us. He'll get lost. And it's cold. And on top of all that . . . we'll have taken his bag.

The only thing left to determine is how on earth we're going to get out without making any noise. In the winter, the cabin tends to shift with the drier weather, making the window frames settle and require extra push just to open them. That extra push is often loud, squeaky like chalk on slate.

I have less than twenty-four hours to come up with something.

Fat snowflakes begin to fall from the sky, and in a matter of minutes, the grass is dusted in white powder. If we're lucky, it'll melt by the time we leave so he won't be able to follow our tracks.

"Is *tee vee* evil?" Sage asks the man as I wash dishes.

I keep my eyes low, trying to ignore the conversation but wondering why she's getting friendly with him. Just because he hasn't harmed us doesn't mean we're friends now or that we're safe.

The man rests his head on his hand, yawning. I'm not sure why he's so tired all the time, but I'm hoping that'll work to our advantage come tomorrow night.

"The government regulates it," he answers. "But there's some bad stuff on TV, that's for sure. Things that would scare you girls."

Years ago, Mama and I were talking about the kinds of things she did for fun when she was a little girl, and she mentioned something called *cartoons* that she would watch on her family's *television set*—TV for short. She said TV started out wholesome and family oriented, and then it became violent and inappropriate, and in the process, it taught people to be violent and inappropriate.

"The government?" I ask.

"Yep," he says. "The FCC."

Mama also once said our government fell apart.

She said we used to have leaders and presidents who wanted to do great things for our country and its people. We revolted, she said, when we realized they lied. Our functional democracy disintegrated, and everything stopped working. There were no presidents, no political parties, no nothing . . . just local municipalities ensuring roads were paved and taxes were collected.

Mama told me all this during our history lessons.

"The FCC?" I ask.

"Federal Communications Commission," he says. "They're in charge of what is and isn't allowed on TV."

"Who's in charge of them?" I ask.

The man's face winces. "I don't know. The president? The senate?"

Mama said we hadn't had a president in decades.

"How do I know you're not making this up?" I ask.

"Making what up?"

"The president." I clear my throat.

"What reason would I have to lie to you about the president and the FCC?" He laughs, lifting up his cell phone. "If this thing had any kind of service out here, I'd look it up on my phone just to prove it to you. Maybe when we get to town in a couple of days. You'll have to remind me."

He doesn't understand my question and I don't understand how his phone could prove the answer, but I let it go.

Turning away from him, I'm elbow deep in cold, soapy water, but I don't feel a thing. Staring through the window above the sink, toward the weeping willow grave site, I can't help but wonder if Mama lied.

CHAPTER 18

Nicolette

"You look rested." Brant smiles from his end of the phone as we video chat the next morning. "Everything going all right back home?"

"Why wouldn't it be?" I wink and ensure that my tone is pleasant so that he has nothing more to worry about, no reason to try to keep pushing me toward Cate.

"Check out this view." He changes the subject, turning his phone toward his hotel room window, showing me an emerald paradise with a gentle river cutting through it. "The Amazon."

I don't know what to say. It's picturesque, of course, but it would be more beautiful in person, and not seeing it in person is a reminder that I'm here, back home, in a gray, wintry northern state, and I'm only here because of something he did.

"When do you have to go shoot?" I ask him as I take a sip of my coffee. The plate of fresh melon and strawberries and hot buttered toast sitting beside me has turned to room temperature, my appetite non-existent. I prepared my breakfast out of habit, as if my subconscious is longing for something normal and familiar to hold on to, but now it's nothing more than a waste.

"In about an hour," he says, checking his watch—the one I gave him on our first anniversary. It still looks new, the leather of the band oiled regularly and the crystal free from scratches. If only he'd put that much love and care into the important things . . . "I'm going to meet another photog for breakfast in the lobby."

I pause for a second, swallowing all the things I *really* want to say. "You didn't tell me there were going to be other photographers there."

"There are tons." He smiles, face lit. Overcompensating, maybe? "I swear I told you this, Nic. *Nat Geo* magazine wants to see how different photographers capture the rain forest through their own lenses. It's a huge project. Remember . . . we talked about it a few months ago?"

Now that he mentions it, I vaguely recall him bringing it up over dinner one evening, but I was only half listening because I figured I'd be in Florida by then and the details wouldn't matter.

Exhaling, I wish to myself that I could stop looking for invisible cracks and pin-size holes in everything he tells me, in everything he does, but until I have answers, I imagine this will be my new normal.

"Right, right," I say, forcing a smile into my tone to counteract my implied accusation from a moment ago.

"Anyway, I should get going." He moves the phone around with him as he slips into shoes, and I have to look away so I don't get dizzy from the blur of colors happening on the screen. He sure seems to be in a hurry. "Can't wait to come home. Miss you already."

He steadies the phone and flashes his handsome smile, the one that used to make my knees buckle and my insides flutter. The one that made me miss him so much it physically hurt—even if he was only on the other side of the room.

Those were the days . . .

"When I get back, maybe we can go away for a while? You and me? Someplace warm?" Even from his perch light-years away, he won't stop looking at me like I'm two seconds from falling apart.

Maybe I am.

And maybe he sees that.

Glancing out the picture windows that flank our fieldstone fireplace, I stare into a desolate forest void of leaves, void of color, void of life.

As soon as I hang up, I'm going to make an appointment with my doctor. I'm going to need my meds bumped up to get through this winter because I'm not going anywhere. I'm going to keep digging, turning over rock after rock, until I uncover the truth.

I know it's out there . . .

And something tells me it's hiding in plain sight.

Scrolling through my contacts, I stop when I get to Dr. Dewdney, my attention caught on the name above.

Davis Gideon—my brother-in-law.

I haven't seen or spoken with him since the last time he was over for dinner, when he'd overdone it on the alcohol and made an ass of himself, slurring his words and spewing rudeness at the only two people who had ever been there for him in his nearly forty years.

It was over a lovingly prepared dinner of chicken saltimbocca, porcini and button mushroom risotto, and chilled Riesling that I'd casually mentioned to Davis that Brant and I were thinking of becoming foster parents. Davis almost choked on a sip of the Busch Light he'd brought from home before asking me what made me think I was qualified for something like that.

I discounted his comment, chalking it up to typical Davis behavior. The man lives to stir the pot, loves to get a reaction. Any time spent with him tends to go one of two ways: it's fine, or it isn't. Most of the time we disregard his attention-seeking behavior, but Brant couldn't ignore this one.

My husband made him leave after that, taking his keys, calling him a ride, and sitting with him outside until he was picked up because, ever the loyal brother, he still couldn't bring himself to completely abandon Davis in his time of need.

The moment was as sweet as it was heartbreaking.

I stayed in the house, cleaning up the dinner mess, trying in vain to make sense of my brother-in-law's remark before deciding it was a giant waste of time because he's . . . Davis.

And Davis says a lot of things.

When my brother-in-law had finally left and my husband returned inside, I told him he didn't have to do that. He stopped before me, looking for a moment as if he was about to say something profound.

His hand lifted.

And fell.

And then he trudged upstairs to his studio, where he stayed until well past midnight.

I haven't brought it up since, and we never discussed it after that. It seemed pointless and masochistic to give weight to a drunkard's opinion.

My husband is a forgiving soul and I've never known him to hold a grudge for very long, but Davis had crossed a line I'd never known existed for Brant: mocking my desire to care for a child.

Still, though. It isn't like Davis to go this long without reaching out and asking for "gas money" or for Brant to "slip him a hundred bucks till payday." Usually we'd hear from him at least once a month. But now? Radio silence. Several months' worth.

Then again, perhaps Davis has been reaching out to Brant, and Brant has failed to mention it for reasons I can only hope are noble.

As an only child, I won't pretend to know the intricacies of sibling relationships, and theirs is only compounded by a less-than-ideal childhood riddled with abusive parents, foster homes, and the sorts of things that can snap a human soul in two if you think about them too long.

I place my phone down, nibble my thumbnail, and lose myself in thought long enough to reach a decision—and a risky one at that.

First thing in the morning, I'll head out to Davis's place, a check in hand and a few questions at the ready. I've witnessed enough over the years to learn there's not much he won't do for a few dollars, and if I add enough zeroes, I might be able to get him to squeal on his brother.

Who knows? He might not know a damn thing.

But odds are . . . he knows *something*.

CHAPTER 19

Wren

That tree's been taunting me since yesterday—the tree that shades the earth that covers the remains of Daddy and Imogen.

This may be morbid, but I have to know. I have to prove to myself that Mama isn't a liar. And there's only one way to find out.

Mama always told me Imogen died before I was born—an accident, she said, never saying a whole lot beyond that because it made her lose her breath and break down into tears every time she thought about it too much.

I don't remember Daddy, though he had to have been in my life at some point. I was one year old when Sage was born, but it's the strangest thing because I can't put a face to my father no matter how hard I try. I used to lie in bed some nights, fighting through the fog of memories as if I could find him if I looked hard enough.

But it never happened.

Mama said most people don't remember the earliest years of their childhood, and she always told me not to feel bad if I couldn't picture his face or remember the Woody Guthrie songs he used to sing when he'd entertain us while Mama was cleaning the kitchen after dinner.

Mama said he died in the forest just past our property line, that someone with a gun shot him and left him for dead. She never knew why, and she never knew who. All by herself, she dragged him back home and buried him under the tree alongside their firstborn.

Sometimes I think I remember that time in our life.

Other times I think they're just those "false memories" Mama always talked about, images my mind created to illustrate Mama's vivid stories.

I'm supposed to be gathering eggs for breakfast, but this morning I've taken a detour to the garden shed in search of a shovel.

Rifling through the garden tools, I find a hoe and a watering can and a hand rake . . . but no shovel.

He must have hidden it, thinking we might use it on him.

Grabbing the hand rake, I march out of the shed, letting the door bang against the side behind me, and I run to the weeping willow tree, falling to my knees in front of the empty flower bed surrounded by rocks the size of my head.

Plunging the rusted tines into the cold, hard dirt, I rake clumps of rock and clay and soil. I'm barely making progress, but I refuse to stop even if the cold air burns my lungs and I have to fight just to take a breath.

Eventually, I toss the hand rake aside, deeming it useless, and I dig into the earth with my bare hands like an animal—wild and determined.

Nothing else matters.

The wind kisses my face, blowing my hair into my eyes, and when I brush it away with my forearm, I'm left with a wet mark. I didn't realize I was crying.

"What . . . are you doing?" The man's voice sends a shock to my heart, and I freeze. "You burying a bone or something?"

He chuckles, and for a moment, I think I might be safe—that he's not going to punish me for taking a detour on my way to gather eggs.

"My father and sister," I say. "I wanted to see if they were really buried here."

Glancing up at him, I squint against the sun. He lifts his hand to his face, massaging his leathery cheek.

"You think your mama lied to you?" he asks.

"I don't know. That's why I'm digging." I pick up the little rake, bracing myself for the moment he tries to yank it out of my hands.

Without saying another word, the man walks away. I don't question it; I don't try to understand it; I only keep digging.

A few minutes later, my dress is stained with earth and my nails are caked with muck, and I stop to catch my breath and examine my progress. The odds of me finishing this on my own without the proper tools aren't good, but I need to keep going.

Gathering what's left of my strength, I plunge the metal into the dirt again and again, stopping only when a familiar metallic chink in my ear pulls my attention to the right.

Our yellow garden shovel stands, driven into the ground, the man's meaty fists clenched around the rubber handle.

"Thought you could use this," he says, his kindness equally appreciated and confusing. I'm not sure where he hid it on our property, but that's the least of my concerns.

Rising, I clap the dirt off my hands before taking the shovel from him and sinking it into the small hole I've already made.

Over and over, I shovel heaps of dirt, piling it into one giant mound, and when I need to stop and take a break, I collapse on the ground and bury my head in my hands, letting the shovel fall at my side. My body aches, joints throbbing and muscles pulsing.

And then I hear the chink of the shovel against rocks and dirt once more.

The stranger has taken over for me . . .

He grunts with each dig, saying nothing.

I catch my breath, silent and watching.

And when he's done, I have my answer.

There are no bones buried here, under the weeping willow, beside the flower bed.

It's nothing but dirt.

Mama lied . . .

Mama *lied*.

◆ ◆ ◆

Sage heats scraps of yesterday's goat meat over the fire, and I pray we don't get sick.

"Why don't you let me take over for a bit?" I ask with a prying smile. Sage loves to cook, but I need to do this. It's part of my plan. It's the only way I'm going to get us out of here.

"But I like cooking," she says.

"Sage," I say under my breath, "you're not used to cooking goat meat. Let me take it from here. Go and grab a can of green beans from the cellar."

Wiping her hands on her apron, she gives me a cockeyed look before asking the stranger if she can go to the cellar. While they're distracted, I lower the pan closer to the fire.

I need the smell of burnt meat.

I need smoke.

I need a reason to have to open the window above the sink.

My sister runs off to the cellar, and the stranger riffles through his bag. I've been paying closer attention lately to the things he keeps in there, and every so often, I watch him fill his empty canteens and jars with well water and pack them in his bag—the bag he needs in order to survive the forest.

Sage returns just as the meat over the fire begins to blacken and shrivel. My gaze moves from her to the stranger to the pan over the fire. A moment later, the meat begins to sizzle and pop, and it doesn't take long until the cabin is filled with haze.

"Wren!" My sister runs toward the fire. "You're burning it!"

I throw my hands in the air, shrieking, and run to the kitchen window, throwing open the sash and sliding the lower half up while the stranger gets the other windows. Sage fans the smoke away, and while the two of them are preoccupied, I swipe a finger full of goat's-milk butter I'd intentionally left out and grease the window—a little trick I learned from this *Bony-Legs* book Mama used to read us.

Tonight when we leave, he won't be able to hear the creak of the window as we slide up the frame.

"I'm so sorry," I say when the chaos settles. "I wasn't paying attention."

The stranger huffs, shaking his head the way Mama does when Evie leaves her dominoes out or Sage forgets to clean up her puzzles.

Sage keeps a close watch on the meat this time, and I take the jar of green beans and begin preparing them . . . keeping the man's portion separate.

Grabbing three tin plates from the shelf, I divvy up the cold beans—a quick heating over the flames should warm them enough—and I take good care to ensure his portion is sprinkled with the melatonin and valerian root I prepared earlier. I'd crushed them so fine the resulting powders were almost invisible, and with salt and pepper, they should be almost tasteless.

Watching the two of them from the corner of my eye, I ensure no one's the wiser, and I get started.

If he finds out what I did . . . he'll kill us both, I'm sure of it.

◆ ◆ ◆

After dinner, the man grabs a book from his bag, some stubby paperback with huge letters on the front, and he rocks in a chair by the fire while we clean up.

Pulling a slate and piece of white chalk from between two dishes where I'd hidden it earlier, I write my sister a silent note: WE'RE LEAVING TONIGHT. AFTER HE FALLS ASLEEP.

Sage's eyes grow wide and for a second she looks like she's about to say something, but she stops herself, knowing better than to make a sound. And this is exactly why I waited until zero hour to tell her any of this. Had I told her earlier, she'd have slipped up or acted unusual all day, and he'd have been onto us.

I couldn't risk it, not when our lives depend on it.

Swiping my hand across the slate, I erase the message and write another one: DRESS IN LAYERS UNDER YOUR NIGHTSHIRT. DON'T MAKE IT OBVIOUS.

I erase that one and scribble a new one: WHATEVER YOU DO, DON'T MAKE A SOUND, DON'T QUESTION ME, AND JUST DO WHAT I SAY.

I run a wet rag across the chalkboard, removing all hints of words left behind, and I slide it behind the sink, out of sight, returning to the dishes as if we'd never stopped. By the time we're finished, the man has stopped rocking in the chair long enough to release an audible yawn.

My breath halts as I observe him from the corner of my eye, watching as he creases the corner of his page and closes his book. A second later, he rises, stretching his arms over his head, and then he heads outside to relieve himself.

Anytime he needs to go number one, he steps outside the front door and walks around to the back of the house, as if taking a quick jaunt to the outhouse is too risky for him.

When the stranger returns, he shoves Mama's bed into place, blocking the door once more, and shrugs out of his flannel shirt.

"Tomorrow we leave," he says, words slow and voice heavy. "First thing. I suggest you two get some sleep. We've got a lot of miles to cover."

Heading to the wardrobe, Sage meets my gaze with a nod before pulling open a door for concealment. Peeling out of the day's clothes, she begins to dress in layers, just as I instructed her—a camisole first, followed by a woolen sweater and knit stockings. When she's finished, she tugs a white nightshirt over her head to hide it all.

I do the same.

He's snoring by the time we're dressed.

The strap of his bag hangs over the edge of Mama's bed, hooked onto one of the posts, and a lump forms in my throat when I think about me trying to grab it and him waking up, but I have to go for it. There's no other option.

"Shoes and coat," I mouth to Sage, pointing to where we keep them.

Tiptoeing across the room, I reach for the black leather band, attempting to lift it with slow, careful effort. Only it's heavier than it looks. Releasing a gentle breath, I try again, the rhythmic snort of his breathing my only reassurance that it's safe to do so.

When I glance at Sage, she waves her hands as if she wants me to hurry up. Summoning all my strength, I hoist the bag up one last time—so slowly my muscles quaver—and exhale when I free it from the post.

Slipping it over my shoulders, I'm almost positive this thing weighs as much as Evie, but I don't have time to think about that.

Pointing to the greased kitchen window, I head in that direction, dragging a throw blanket off my bed on the way and placing it over a chair to muffle any sounds should it bump against the wall as we climb out.

As soon as everything is in place, I slide the window up and help my sister out first, followed by the bag, which I lower to her.

It falls on the ground with a dead thud after slipping through her waiting arms, and my heart ricochets.

Turning toward the sleeping stranger, I wait, ensuring he's still snoring before I climb the chair and hoist myself out the window.

The cold bites the parts of our flesh left exposed, and only a half moon lights our way.

"I have to lift you," I whisper. "We need to close the window. Slow and quiet, do you understand?"

We have to keep the cabin warm. One cold draft could pull him out of his slumber, and the second he gets up to shut the window, he'll see that we've fled.

Sage bites her bottom lip and nods, and I wrap my arms around her hips, lifting her as high as I can. My muscles shake, barely able to sustain her weight despite her slight size, but within seconds, her willowy fingertips press against the dirty glass, sliding it down without so much as a squeak.

Lowering Sage to the cold earth, I regain my balance before slipping the bag over my shoulders and looping my hand in hers.

"Ready?" My voice is whisper soft.

My sister nods.

And then we run.

CHAPTER 20

Nicolette

Davis doesn't use his turn signal as he pulls into his driveway this morning—then again, he wouldn't need to. There are no neighbors for miles. The ruts in these dirt-and-gravel county roads leading up to his secluded acreage are his and only his.

The clock on my dash reads 8:54 AM, which confirms he's still working nights at the factory in the next town. He's going on three and a half years now of steady employment—a new record.

I kill my engine just as Davis climbs down from his truck and slams the door. It's only when he jerks his head in my direction that I realize he had no idea I'd been behind him for the past couple of miles.

His thick-skinned, sun-spotted hand rubs at his chest as he steps toward my car, and I roll down my window. I don't bother stepping out. I have no intention of making this anything other than a quick and painless-for-him visit. Always a bit of a recluse with hermit tendencies, he's never been a big fan of company. The one time I did stop by unannounced, it was early in my relationship with Brant. I'd brought Davis some leftovers, hoping I could score brownie points with the one family member who seemed to mean anything to my boyfriend at the time. I'll never forget the way he blocked his door with his guarded stance, peering down his nose as if I were Cinderella's evil stepmother delivering a poisoned apple. When I'd told Brant about it later, he said not to take it personally, that his brother didn't like unannounced visits—or most people for that matter.

My visit today is unannounced, but the thousand-dollar personal check resting on my passenger seat should remedy any minor inconvenience this may have caused dear Davis.

"Nicolette." He yanks the dusty ball cap off his thinning head of hair and wipes his forearm against his furrowed brow.

"Do you have a minute?" I ask.

He scoffs. "Do I have a choice?"

I reach for the check, handing it through the open window. He yanks it out of my fingers before examining it.

"What the hell is this?" he asks, chuckling. "Brant know you're out here?"

"He does not." I sit a little straighter and clear my throat. "And I need for it to stay that way."

Davis's gray eyes skim over the check before landing on me, and he forces a huff through half-pursed lips. Folding the check in half, he tucks it into the front left pocket of his blue plaid shirt.

"Aw, don't tell me . . . trouble in paradise?" he asks, though his tone is all amusement and zero concern.

"I need to know what you know." I cut to the chase.

His lips peel apart, revealing his tobacco-stained smile. "You got a lot of nerve, Nicolette. Driving up here in your rich-bitch car, thinking you can wave a check in my face and I'll squeal like a pig."

My chest tightens, and my gaze flicks to the steering wheel for a second before daring to return. I won't let him shake me, even if I hate that he's got a point.

"He's not been himself lately," I say. "I'm just wondering if there's anything you know, anything at all . . . I realize I'm asking the world of you, but you have to understand—your brother . . . he's *my* world."

"Ain't that cute." Davis laughs through his nose before scratching the tip of it with his pointer finger, the nail of which is caked in dirt. "Listen, I don't know what makes you think I know a damn thing about my brother's *dealings*, but he hasn't said a word to me in months. Not since he kicked me out of your *humble* home after asking me over for dinner."

Clearly, Davis is still bitter about that night. And clearly, he's not taking an ounce of responsibility for his behavior—typical.

"If you're asking me if I know if he's stepping out on you, I don't," Davis says, though somehow I don't find the comfort I was hoping for in his revelation. "If you're asking me if I think he ever would . . . I don't know, Nic. Can't imagine it's a walk in the park being married to you."

My fist clenches around the steering wheel. "And what's that supposed to mean?"

I resist the urge to scream at him, to tell him he knows nothing about our marriage. He doesn't know the first thing about love, commitment, or human decency.

"I don't know, just seems like he's always kowtowing to you," he says. "Bending over backward to make sure you have everything you need, making sure you don't have another one of your episodes."

He lifts a hand, curled fingers insinuating air quotes around the word "episodes."

I've heard enough.

Davis is either lying and covering for his brother or he's truly just as in the dark as I am. Either way, he's not the wealth of information I'd hoped he'd be.

"Screw you, Davis." I start my car and check the rearview mirror, though the latter move is unnecessary. Davis has no visitors, no friends. He's an island, though he's more like that island of trash that floats around the Atlantic Ocean. No one wants him. No one knows what to do with him.

"I'm cashing the check." He pats his pocket as I shift into reverse.

Fair enough.

That's what I get for trying to make a deal with the devil.

Backing onto the dusty road, I shift into drive and head home, bank account a little lighter but mind just as heavy.

◆ ◆ ◆

"Hey, Nicki girl." My lifelong best friend singsongs my name into the phone later that afternoon. "Just checking on you."

I roll my eyes. Cate means well, but I don't need to be checked on. I'm not a child staying home alone while my parents jet off to some exotic locale.

"I'm *fine*," I say.

"It's so weird not having you here," she says. "I had all these plans for us for New Year's."

"I know. I'm sorry. I wish I was there, I really do."

"So why aren't you?" Her question is serious, but she laughs through her nose. "I don't understand why you all of a sudden want to spend winter in that frozen tundra hellhole. No offense. I know how much you hate winters up there."

"I see you've been talking to Brant."

She pauses. "More like *he's* been talking to *me*."

"He called you?"

The sound of rustling papers and slamming desk drawers answers me before she does. She must be working. "He did. But only because he was concerned for you."

I drag my hands through my hair before clasping my hand across my forehead and resting my elbows on my knees.

I can't get comfortable lately.

Can't sit still.

Can't just . . . be.

"Cate, he's making something out of nothing. I'll be fine up here. I promise." I don't need to be treated with kid gloves, and I don't need to be made into some crazy person just because I have a little seasonal depression. By the time spring rolls around, I'm usually down to one antidepressant a day and back to appreciating life again. "I get that you two worry about me, but you're both overreacting."

I bury my disappointment with Cate because I know she's coming from a good place and she has no idea what's behind my decision to stay, but she knows me better than anyone—maybe even better than my husband—since we've been friends nearly our entire lives, our families summering together in Nantucket since our grade-school years. She should know me enough to trust me and to let it go.

"Maybe I can come up there?" Cate asks. "Just for a week or two. Or three. If I'm feeling masochistic."

She snickers.

"You *hate* it up here," I say.

"Yeah, but I love hanging out with my best friend, so those two things basically cancel each other out."

"Fine," I say, a tease in my tone. "I'll allow it."

"I want the big guest room, though," she says. "The one with the soaker tub."

"I'll have to make sure that one's available, but we should be able to accommodate you."

She laughs. "Glad to see you haven't completely lost your sense of humor."

"Why would I?"

Cate hesitates for a moment. "I don't know . . . you just seem . . . down lately. Off. I don't know how to describe it. When I talk to you on the phone, you just seem more distant. Like you're not you. And Brant notices it, too. Thought maybe you're slipping into—"

"Cate." I say her name with a groan. We've taken ten steps backward here. "Please stop worrying about me, book your damn flight, and get your fine self out here so I can see what you look like without that everlasting tan of yours."

I manage to get a slight chuckle out of her. "I don't even think I know what my actual skin color is anymore."

"So come find out."

"Fine," she says, a smile in her tone. "I'll look at tickets as soon as we hang up."

"Thank you," I say with the teasing arrogance of someone who just won an argument.

She's quiet for a moment. So am I.

"Nic?" she asks.

"Yes?"

"You'd tell me if something was going on with you, right?" she asks, clearly in the mood to beat a dead horse.

"Just . . . we can talk more when you get here." I shut my eyes tight.

"I *knew* it," she says. "Oh, God. Something's wrong. What is it?"

"I don't know, Cate . . . I don't know."

She sucks in a quick breath, releasing it into the receiver. "You're scaring me."

"I'm looking into some things," I confess, though I won't elaborate until she's here, until I can tell her these things in person. "Until I know more, I don't want to say anything. But that's why I'm staying here."

Cate's silent, which is unusual, and I can almost picture her pacing her terra-cotta tile floors, nibbling on her hot-pink manicure.

"Nic . . ." Cate's voice falls. "At least tell me if it's Brant. If you two can't make it, there's no hope for the rest of us."

"Can we talk about this another time?" I ask. "Like when you're here?"

"Yeah, of course," she says, speaking slowly as if she's still trying to process this information. "I'm booking that flight tonight. I promise. I'll text you the details."

"Perfect."

Cate is quiet once again, then she exhales into her receiver.

"What?" I ask.

"This is really going to bother me." Her tone is teasing yet not. "And I'm going to be up all night worrying now."

"Please don't," I say. At this point, I'm doing enough worrying for the both of us. "Just book that flight, and we'll chat more when you get here."

I use the word "chat" over "talk" in hopes it'll quell her worries. Chats are fun and casual. You only have a "talk" when things are about to get real.

I hang up with my best friend and reach for the glass of Pinot Noir to my right, the one sitting beside the half-finished bottle. To my left lies our wedding album. Something about finding my marriage potentially on shaky ground makes me want to comb through the entirety of our relationship, examining all the bits and pieces and corners and crevices, scrutinizing every memory to ensure we were truly happy from the very beginning and that it wasn't all in my head.

In perfect clarity, I can still recall the moment he walked into the Berkshire Gallery. Approaching the front desk, he stated his name and that he had an appointment with Mr. Berkshire. There was nothing out of the ordinary about our little exchange except for the way he looked at me—pure captivation. I remember losing my breath but being physically unable to look away from those piercing eyes, bright like a green variation of turquoise but soft like sea glass. And his hair, sandy blond, with tendrils that hung over his forehead.

That man was a work of art himself, more wondrous than any of the art adorning the stark white walls of our galleria. And within a matter of seconds, I managed to convince myself that he probably looked at *all* women that way. Men like him—the ones with the breathtakingly unfair good looks—were as prevalent as the giant rats that inhabited the subway system and the five-foot-eleven Eastern European beauties who came to the city in hopes of signing with Wilhelmina or IMG.

They were just a part of the landscape, a part of the culture here. You only really noticed them if you were looking for them, and Lord knows I wasn't looking for this one.

Mr. Berkshire came out a second later, our moment suspended, and as soon as they disappeared upstairs, Marin told me Brant Gideon was the next hot thing—and she would've known. She had her ear to the ground in the New York art scene, and I was nothing but a naive twenty-two-year-old with a shiny new art history degree, the ink barely dry on my diploma.

When Brant came out of his meeting, he wasted no time asking for my number and securing a date for Friday night at some cozy, off-the-radar hot spot in the East Village. All I remember is wanting to say no and to seem aloof and uninterested, but my heart was galloping so fast I couldn't think straight so Marin answered for me.

I didn't know it then, but he would propose to me right there, in that East Village bar, exactly one year later. A year after that, he would marry me at my parents' estate in Nantucket, swearing his undying love to me in front of 624 guests, refusing to let his new bride out of his sight for a single second the entirety of the evening. And when the night was over, he slipped my heels off my tired feet and carried me to a waiting car that whisked us off to a waterfront hotel room, where we somehow found the energy to make love not once but twice and then again the next morning, before our flight left for the first leg of our European honeymoon.

We were happy then. I refuse to believe we weren't.

Flipping through our photos, I linger on each and every one until the nostalgia hits me with a burst of both blissful longing and undeniable sadness, and then I move to the next. Our smiles were giant, our eyes sparkly and full of life. Napping under the Eiffel Tower in Paris. Sleeping in an Irish castle. Cliff jumping in Finland. Our honeymoon, in all its magical bliss, is all there, fully documented. When I get to the end of the album, I find copies of the vows we'd written to each other.

Pulling his from the protective sleeve, I reread the words, his neat, tight handwriting with exaggerated loops filling the space of a five-by-eight slip of linen heirloom paper.

Nicolette,

I never believed in love at first sight, and I never thought I was the marrying type . . . but then I met you, and everything I thought I knew about myself changed. Just like that. Let me first say, shamelessly and unapologetically, that it was your beauty that caught my attention at first. But by the end of our first date, I knew you were so much more than your sapphire starlight eyes and your contagious laugh and your grace and intelligence.

I couldn't get enough of you. I don't know that forever would ever be long enough together, but there's only one way to find out . . .

I carried your ring around in my pocket for months before I had the nerve to ask you to marry me. While I was certain you'd say yes because by then we were in the throes of something so perfect and so right, part of me was terrified you'd say no and that I'd have to live my life without you—which at the time seemed like a death sentence.

But one night we walked past a Cartier window and you stopped by the rings, pausing for just a second when you thought I wasn't looking, and I knew.

I knew you'd say yes.

So I asked the next month. And you said yes. And now here we are.

So, Nic, because you've made my dreams come true, the least I can do is promise the same to you.

From this day on, you have me. You have my love. My support. My honesty. My trust. You have everything you could ever need from me and more. All you have to do is say the word, and it's yours.

Your happiness is my happiness, now and forever.

That is my vow to you, my darling.

I return the vows to the back pocket of the album and close the binding. Taking another sip of wine, I stare ahead at the crackling fireplace across from me, thinking of how he used to call me his "darling" and wondering when it was that he stopped.

I can't remember.

What else have I forgotten?

CHAPTER 21

Wren

My feet burn with every step, my ankles growing weak and threatening to roll as we navigate through towering pines. My knees are skinned from falling over broken tree branches halfway through our journey, but we stopped only long enough for me to catch my breath. The trickle of moonlight through the treetops barely lights our way. For all I know, we're running in circles, but hours ago, I drew an imaginary line between the moon and myself, and that's the direction I'm taking us.

"Wren." Sage calls my name, her voice breathy and barely there. "Wren, I need to stop."

Slowing down, I reach back, wrapping my fingers around her bony wrist. "We can't."

We stop, we die.

I have no idea when the stranger will wake, but I imagine when he does, he'll waste no time trying to track us down, and our footsteps will point him in a general direction.

We left him for dead. If he meant it when he said he didn't want to kill us before . . . I imagine this will change his mind.

"Wren, please . . ." My sister's plea is followed with a soft whimper, and she yanks her hand from my grasp.

Left with no choice but to stop, I turn to her, watching as she lowers herself to the cold, hard earth.

"I'm so tired," she says, her lip quivering as dead leaves crunch and rustle beneath her. "I'm cold. And I'm hungry. And . . . I'm scared."

Lowering myself, I place my hands on her fragile shoulders. I'm all those things, too, but I can't let her know. One of us has to be strong.

"I miss Mama." She buries her head in her hands before wiping glistening tears on the backs of her hands.

Throwing my arms around her, I pull her in, taking in the wild beat of her terrified little heart and the tiny shudders that follow each jagged breath.

Leaving our home for the first time is nothing short of terrifying, but we can't succumb to that if we want to live . . . if we want to get away from that man . . . and find Mama.

This is the only way.

"I know you're scared, Sage," I whisper, "but we have to keep going."

She dries her tears once more and locks her dark eyes on mine. "How much longer?"

Exhaling, I shake my head. "I don't know."

Pushing herself off the ground, she dusts off her coat, and I do the same, my joints tightening and the backs of my heels burning like fire. I didn't know how badly my feet were hurting until we stopped moving.

"You want a drink of water?" I ask, digging around in the stranger's bag. We haven't stopped for food and drink except once tonight, when Sage had to relieve herself. It was then that I found small packets of nuts and seeds, dried berries and raisins buried deep in the stranger's bag. Pulling out one of the many canteens the man had packed over the past few days, I unscrew the lid and hand it over. "Here. Quick."

The sky has lightened since we stopped, and the sun should be up soon. The thought of losing our cover of darkness makes my stomach churn, but I force it away.

Sage brings the water to her lips before hesitating.

"Hurry," I tell her, glancing up at the darkness that fades to baby blue.

"Wren." Her voice is a cracked murmur, and her slender fingers grip my shoulder. "Look."

Sage's arm lifts, her finger pointed, and I follow her gaze toward a break in the forest where a large structure sits, so real, so clear. There's a porch along the side facing us. Bright lights, almost like little kerosene lamps but brighter, flank the shiny glass windows. We must have missed it before, when the sun had yet to rise.

"Come on." I slink her limp arm around my shoulders and brace her exhausted body as we tromp over snapped twigs and rotting leaves and fallen pine cones.

The closer we get, the more enormous the structure becomes. Mama always said everyone's homesteads were different, some being humbler than others, but until this moment, I could only ever imagine variations of our cabin.

But this . . . this is not a cabin.

With its straight lines and polished exterior and abundance of windows, I wouldn't know what to call it.

Leading my sister to the property's edge, I emerge from the dark cocoon of the Stillwater Forest. Hand in hand, we amble toward a walkway made of stone that leads straight to the door of an unfamiliar homestead.

The only thing I can do now is pray that the people who live here are good people who do nice things and don't hurt others.

I would never forgive myself if I led us out of a lion's den and into a bobcat's lair.

CHAPTER 22

Nicolette

Standing in front of the bathroom sink, I stare at a stranger's reflection, tracing my fingertips along the bags forming beneath her bloodshot eyes. If I didn't know this woman, I might feel sorry for her, but I've never been a fan of self-pity.

Exhaustion paints my face in unflattering colors, but it's nothing a cold compress can't soothe and a little concealer can't hide.

I stayed up way too late last night, poring over photographs and recalling happier times, masochistically trying to figure out if I could have seen this coming and if I somehow chose to ignore it.

Sleep came before I was able to make a determination.

While Brant clearly knows who this girl is and has chosen to hide her photo from me, my mother always said it's dangerous to walk around making assumptions. But those eyes . . . those sea-glass eyes that match Brant's fleck for fleck . . . I can't get them out of my head.

Cupping a handful of lukewarm water between my palms, I rinse my face and pat my skin dry before heading downstairs for a cup of coffee.

I've stayed home from Brant's work trips plenty of times over the course of our marriage and for various reasons, but this particular instance feels different. The echoes in our home are a little more pronounced. The sound of my footsteps slightly louder. The howling of the wind more noticeable. All of it serves to remind me that it's just me out here, alone, next to these deep woods and under this gray sky on a road that's lucky to see any traffic besides our own on a typical day.

Pulling a mug from the cupboard, I slip my thumb through the ceramic handle and shuffle to the built-in coffee station in the butler's pantry. Not in the mood for sweets, I take it black.

"Hello?"

A voice so meek I'm positive I'm imagining it floats through my home, nearly causing me to spill my drink, so I place it aside and angle my ear toward the next room. My breath suspends, and I brace myself against the soapstone pantry counter. Sometimes the wind howls so hard out here it can sound like someone's at the door, but it's always nothing.

No one comes here unless they have to.

And I certainly can't blame them. We're impossible to find. Hours from the city or any ounce of culture. When the weather's bleak, it's unbearably cold. When it's warm, we're surrounded by mosquitoes and cicadas chirruping so loud you need earmuffs to sleep at night.

My parents visit at scheduled increments, mostly birthdays or holidays, and Brant's brother used to come for dinner every so often—before their falling-out several months ago.

Holding my breath, I listen to the nothingness that fills my house, trying to decide if that "hello" I heard a moment ago was nothing more than a figment of my imagination. I shake my head and reach for my coffee. Why I would even assume that someone would randomly show up at my door at 7:00 AM unannounced is beyond me.

Heading to the kitchen, I take a seat at the table and stare out the floor-to-ceiling window toward the sparse trees that surround our home.

In the springtime, the woods surrounding Stillwater Hills are full of life and perfectly formed by Mother Nature herself. They serve as home to the most magnificent flora and fauna: primroses and monarchs in the spring, golden chanterelle mushrooms in the summer, and plums and persimmons in the fall.

But in the winter? The forest is nothing more than a rotting, half-functioning wind block of the eyesore variety.

Brant always said everything has to die to be reborn again, but I beg to differ. There are plenty of places on this earth with lush green everything always, places where nothing dies because the sun refuses not to shine.

Lifting my mug, I take a sip.

"Hello?"

A splash of black liquid sloshes over the edge of my cup when I place it aside.

There's a knock next.

Followed by an undeniable "Hello?" this time.

Steadying my breath, I step lightly toward the security system control center in the hallway, pressing the code and pulling up the camera views to check the outside of the house. The garage camera shows an empty driveway. The camera angled toward the backyard and the wraparound porch shows the same: nothing and no one. Pressing the front porch option, I squint, studying the two dark masses standing in front of my door until they come into focus.

Gasping, I cup a clammy hand over my chest.

Taking a closer look at the security camera, I zoom in on the faces of the two figures.

Girls.

The image of two young girls with hollowed eyes and gaunt faces, long, unkempt hair dripping down their shoulders, one blonde, one brunette, is as haunting as it is real. The blonde is taller but not by much, and her arm is hooked over the smaller one's shoulders.

The camera's focus isn't the best in this light, a little grainy and delayed by two seconds, but it doesn't take much to see they're both shivering.

Three raps echo through the house, sending my heart knocking in my chest harder than before. This could be a setup. I've heard of dubious people feigning to be stranded motorists or pretending to be injured, all in an attempt to rob someone. There could be others hiding around the side of the house, out of sight of the cameras, well aware that I'd have to disarm the system in order to open the door, and that's when they'd strike.

I try to assure myself that if anything happens, if these girls are simply lures and someone else tries to intrude, all I'd have to do is press a button on the keypad, the alarm will sound, and the police will be here in less than ten minutes.

Brant has a gun upstairs in a safe in his closet. It's just a handgun, small enough to hide in his palms. I've never used it before, but it's still a deterrent if it comes to that.

"We need help," the voice from outside my door says. "Please . . ."

The temperature on the monitor's screen reads twenty-three degrees—well below freezing.

I stare at the live footage, watching, paralyzed. Moments later, the smaller one presses her head against the other's shoulder, her face wincing as if she's in pain.

The fair-haired girl knocks again, this time harder.

Dragging in a heavy breath, I pad to the kitchen to grab my phone and dial 911.

"911, what's your emergency?" The dispatcher answers on the first ring.

"Hi, yes, this is Nicolette Gideon," I say, injecting all the calm I can muster into my tone. "Four seven nine Orchid Drive. There are two young girls outside on my doorstep asking for help. They appear to be . . . *not well.* Can you send someone right away, please?"

"Yes, Ms. Gideon," she says, the faint sound of her keyboard clicking in the background. "Are they physically injured in any way?"

"I . . . I don't know. I haven't answered the door," I say, knowing full well I'm putting my spinelessness out there. "I just woke up a little while ago and heard them outside asking for help. I live just outside of town, miles from the nearest neighbor. It's so early, and this is so unusual. I guess I just wanted to be—"

Justifying my cowardice isn't my finest moment.

"Ma'am, it's fine. I'm sending someone out right now. We'll send medical, too," she says. "Stay put. And let me know if they leave, okay?"

"I will." Heading to the door, I glance out the peephole and see that they're still there.

"I'll stay on the line until the responding officer arrives," she says.

I clutch the phone against my chest, hands trembling so hard I almost drop it on the foyer floor.

The girls haven't budged.

They're not giving up, not leaving.

Desperation breeds resilience, but then again, so can evil.

From here, I get a better look at their clothes. Tattered, faded dresses with dirty hems protrude out from the bottom of their long, brown coats, and their feet are covered in stained boots.

I don't know any teenagers around here who'd be caught dead dressing like that.

My hand clenches the doorknob, and every part of me wants to help them more than it wants to fear them. If Brant were here, he'd have opened the door by now. He's fearless like that, and on top of that, he's a people pleaser. He wants everyone to like him. He wants to be a hero. And there's no better way to validate your worth than by helping people.

But that's neither here nor there.

"No one's here," the little one says. "We should go."

Checking my phone screen, I see it's only been two minutes. It'll be at least another eight before the police arrive.

Slipping my phone into the left breast pocket of my pajama top, I undo the locks on the door and give the door a gentle pull so as not to startle the girls.

And then I try not to gasp when I take in the disturbing sight before me—the tiny eyes and skin-and-bones features and matted hair sticking out from pilling knit caps. These girls are almost otherworldly and definitely not from around here, at least not that I can surmise.

The blonde one grips the dark-haired one tight, both of them trembling, though from fear or cold I'm not sure.

"H . . . hi," she says, her pale-blue eyes wide and round. "I'm . . . s-sorry to bother you . . ."

Being face-to-face with them, I can't help but find their appearances distracting. The little one stares, unblinking, and I scan the length of her torn patchwork coat, which has been darned and repaired with floral-printed fabric in several places. There's a hole in the toe of her left boot, and a bit of her woolen sock pokes through. Her hair, limp and heavy with natural oils, hangs around her shoulders, tapering to ratted ends that stop past her elbows.

"W . . . we . . . need help," the blonde says. I couldn't begin to guess her age if I tried. She's certainly much too small and shapeless to be an adult, but she's far from a child. Same with the other girl, though there's a sort of quiet, wide-eyed curiosity about her, like a sheltered child seeing everything for the first time.

Moving back, I motion for them to step inside. Holding hands, they cross the threshold of the front door and stand with gaping eyes in the center of our two-story foyer.

"What happened to you?" I ask as gently as possible. "Are you hurt? Do you know where your parents are? Are they looking for you?"

They look so young with their round, innocent eyes, and they haven't stopped shaking despite the seventy-two degrees my thermostat is set at.

They remind me of abandoned baby bunnies . . . sad and sweet and destined to either thrive or die from shock.

"The police are on the way," I say. "Come on in. Have a seat. Are you hungry? Thirsty?"

I lock the door and head toward the kitchen, waving for them to follow. The girls stay several steps behind, but a moment later they stand in the doorway, glued at the hip, as I fill two glasses with water.

"You can have a seat over there." I point to the table. "Are you hungry?"

They say nothing, but their gaunt faces tell me all I need to know. Heading into the pantry, I retrieve a loaf of bread and a jar of peanut butter. From the fridge, I grab strawberry jelly and a bowl of rinsed, seedless grapes.

"They're sending an ambulance, too," I say, fixing their toast and plucking green grapes from their vine. "In case you need medical attention."

The girls haven't said a single word since they stepped inside. They only stare at me with their careful, watchful gazes and clench their bony hands together as they shuffle to the table to take a seat.

"Are you hurt?" I ask again, placing their plates in front of them.

Their sunken eyes inspect the food, but they don't touch it, at least not at first.

"It's okay," the older one whispers to the younger one. "You can eat it. She seems nice."

Nothing about them leads me to believe they're related. The little one has dark, pointed features, and the bigger one has bright, saffron-blonde hair; crystalline-blue, hooded eyes; a round face; and a spray of freckles over her nose.

A lump forms in my throat when I think that I might be sitting across from two victims of child trafficking. Perhaps they escaped? Perhaps they've never known another decent human being, and that's why they're so uncertain of me?

The faint wail of a police siren outside grows louder by the second. The little one is midbite when she stops and turns to the older one.

"It's okay," I tell them, placing my palms up. "It's just the police. They're here to help."

My words don't register, at least not on their heavy-lidded expressions. Their weary appearances lead me to believe they haven't slept in ages. Maybe they're out of it? Maybe they were drugged? Maybe they ran for days and days until they came across my house?

Whatever happened, I'm sure the police will get to the bottom of it.

Flashes of red and blue burst through my windows, and a swift rap at my door comes a few moments later.

Lifting a finger, I smile at the girls. "I'll be right back, okay?"

Heading to the door, I yank it open and find myself standing face-to-face with a female sheriff's deputy in head-to-toe khaki. Her hair is combed back into a low bun, and while the brown-gray of her hair hints at middle age, there isn't so much as a trace of smile lines on her skin.

Removing her hat, she begins to speak, but I cut her off with, "They're in here."

Glancing toward the driveway before closing the door behind her, I spot the ambulance pulling in and crawling to a stop.

"Just this way." I lead her to the kitchen, where the girls are inhaling the remains of their peanut butter and jelly toast. Their two water glasses, which were filled to the top a moment ago, are now empty. All that remains are their untouched grapes. "Girls, this is Deputy . . ." I glance at her name tag. ". . . Deputy May. She's here to help you."

The older girl freezes, still as a statue but eyes live and alert, and the younger one stares down at her lap.

I have a feeling their story won't be for the faint of heart.

"Hi, girls," Deputy May says in a voice as sweet as honey cakes. "Ms. Gideon here gave us a call because she wanted us to make sure you're okay."

The girls deposit their slow, watchful gazes in her direction, but their lips are sealed tight, as if they have no intention of speaking.

"Can you tell me what happened? How you got here?" the deputy asks with a friendly smile.

They say nothing.

"Are either of you hurt?" she asks.

I resist the urge to prompt them to say something. I'm not their mother. I'm simply the woman who answered the door and gave them food and water. They have no reason to do anything I tell them to do.

The dark-haired one reaches for a grape, examining it between her fingers.

"It's okay," the older one says. "You can eat it. We grew those one year, remember? Ours were purple."

The deputy and I exchange looks.

The little one pops it into her mouth, chewing with intention, rolling it around on her tongue and reaching for a second one when she's done.

"I understand you might be scared right now," May says, her hands resting on her duty belt, "but we really want to help you, and we can't do that unless you tell us what happened."

"What are your names?" I ask, hoping desperately to break the ice. Flattening my palm against my chest, I say, "I'm Nicolette."

My eyes lock with the older one. I have every reason to believe she's not going to answer me, so I don't push her.

"You can call me Nic if you'd like," I add with a sweet smile.

The pause between us all lingers, and the sound of Deputy May drawing in a slow breath fills my ears.

"Wren," the blonde girl says. "My name is Wren. And my sister's name is Sage."

So they *are* sisters . . .

Deputy May takes the chair across from them. "And how did you get here, girls?"

"We walked," Wren says. "Can I take off my coat?"

"Of course," I say.

She shrugs out of her threadbare jacket, revealing a pale nightdress drenched in sweat and clinging to her thin frame. I take the jacket from her, draping it over the back of a chair. The overwhelming scent of stale must fills the air.

"Where are you from?" the deputy asks. "Do you know your address?"

Wren squints and then blinks, as if she doesn't understand the question.

"What about your parents?" Deputy May tilts her head. "Are they looking for you?"

Sage glances up at Wren, but Wren doesn't flinch. "No."

"Do you . . . do you have parents?" May asks, thin brows raised.

"We did," Wren says, gaze flicking toward her plate.

For a moment, I'm convinced I'm dreaming because none of this seems real and none of it makes sense, but I take a seat beside the deputy and trust she knows what she's doing, that she knows how to ask the questions in a way to get them to answer.

"Wren, I need to use the outhouse," the little one whispers.

Outhouse?

May forces a hard breath through her nose as we exchange looks.

"I don't have an outhouse," I say with a pillow-soft apology, "but I have a bathroom. It's like an outhouse but with running water and lights." Rising, I add, "I'll walk you there. It's just down the hall."

Sage looks to Wren, and Wren tells her it's all right. A second later, I'm heading to the powder bath in the hall with the little coffee-eyed darling in tow.

Flicking on the light, I step out of the way, only Sage doesn't enter. She stands, staring, her hands pressed against the doorframe.

"Have you ever used a bathroom like this before?" I ask.

She bites her bottom lip and shakes her head once, her eyes moving from the toilet to the faucet to the mirror and then to me.

Moving into the powder room, I lift the lid and say, "This is where you . . . relieve yourself." Pointing to the chrome lever on the back of the tank, I say, "You push this when you're done."

I don't want it to scare her, so I demonstrate, flushing a clean bowl of water and standing back as she watches it swirl around the white porcelain and disappear.

"When you're finished, you wash your hands here." I reach for the faucet handles, turning each one on and then off, and then I point to a white dispenser and the gray hand towel hanging on the bar to the left. "There's your soap. You can dry your hands here when you're done."

"Th . . . thank you," she says, hands folded across her tiny waist.

I step away and return to the kitchen, where Deputy May is walking away from the table, her hand pressed on her radio as she speaks into the mic.

Wren stares ahead, a blank look on her face, and May points me toward a vacant hallway.

"We're going to take them to Mercy General," she says when we're out of Wren's sight. "They'll get a full medical workup, and we'll have psych evaluate them. Child Protective Services is on their way as well."

I'm not sure what I expected, but all this is happening so fast. One minute they're knocking at my door asking for help and shaking like scrawny little leaves; the next minute they're eating like they haven't eaten in years. And the fact that I had to show Sage how to use a modern-day bathroom adds a whole new level of peculiarity to this situation.

"Can I go with them?" I ask.

May raises her left brow.

"I know I don't know them, but they're alone," I say. "They're scared. They should have someone . . . someone who isn't in a uniform . . . someone who can stay with them, answer their questions, tell them everything's going to be okay."

"Ms. Gideon, I appreciate your concern, but—"

"Please," I say, cutting her off. "I won't intervene. I'll stay out of your way—I just . . . I think they need someone who's not on the clock—no offense . . . and right now I'm all they have."

May gives me a tight-lipped smile as if to appease me as she pauses. "All right. Fine. If the girls want you there, you can be there. But you won't be privy to any of their medical data or any nonpublic information related to our investigation."

"I completely understand." I lift my right hand to my heart.

A knock at the front door interrupts our conversation, followed by footsteps a moment later. I glance past her shoulder to find two male deputies trekking across my foyer, their heavy-booted footsteps echoing along with the squawk of their radios.

"In here," May calls, hands moving to her duty belt.

A deafening shriek fills my left ear, coming from the hallway near the powder room, and without pause, I run toward the awful noise only to find Sage slumped up against the wall, her hands cupping her ears and her eyes squeezed tight, wailing.

The two deputies stand over her before glancing to May.

Sage's sister squeezes between them to get to her, and the deputy motions for the men to step away, out of sight.

Wren's lanky arms wrap around Sage, and she whispers something in her ear. A moment later the crying stops, though her chest rises and falls so fast I fear she might hyperventilate.

"Girls . . . *girls*," May says, lowering herself to their level. "What's going on? Those are Deputies Alvarez and Thomason. They're here to help. You have no reason to be scared of them, I promise. They're just going to try to trace your footprints, maybe see if they can find something to help us figure out where you came from."

The little one buries her face into Wren's lithe shoulders, and Wren holds her tight. "She thought . . . she thought it was . . . there was a man . . . at our cabin . . ."

Her voice is shaky and she struggles to finish her thought, so May cuts them off. "It's okay, it's okay. One thing at a time. You don't have to be around men if you don't want to. Once we get to the hospital, we'll request only female doctors and nurses."

May turns, giving me a wordless look as if to suggest this entire thing goes much deeper than either of us could've imagined.

"There are doctors?" Wren asks, brows lifted. "There are doctors at this . . . *hospital*?"

Drying her tears on her sleeve, Sage glances up at her sister. "Wren, maybe Evie is there?"

The deputy's hands rest at her hips. "Who's Evie?"

Wren turns to her. "Our other sister."

May pinches the bridge of her nose. "There are *three* of you?"

Wren nods. "Evie was sick. Mama took her to town to see if a doctor could help her. That was months ago. They never came back."

May's hands rest on her hips, and the elevens between her eyebrows deepen. The four of us bask in a soundless moment until someone calls May on the radio and she walks into the next room as she responds. A moment later she returns.

"We should go now," she says. "The hospital's expecting us."

◆ ◆ ◆

"I'm with them." I point to the girls and Deputy May once I arrive at the main desk at Mercy General.

May nods, waving me over.

The ride to town was silent in an eerie sort of way yet kissed with the warm glow of a late-winter sunrise filtering through barren landscapes. It seemed fitting, like a grim illustration that could be interpreted twenty different ways.

Wren and Sage rode in the back of Deputy May's cruiser, and I followed in my SUV. From a few car lengths back, I watched as the two of them wrapped their arms around each other, occasionally staring back at me with their hollow eyes.

I imagine they're terrified.

A young nurse in pink scrubs with a tight blonde ponytail emerges from behind an automatic door, her wide gaze honing in on the girls.

"It's okay. She's a nurse," May says. "She's come to take you back."

Wren turns to me. "Will you come with us?"

I glance at the deputy. "If Deputy May says it's all right."

May nods, and while I'm sure it isn't protocol, the situation is unique enough that I imagine she's willing to put her neck out there to ensure the girls have whatever they need to feel comfortable enough to cooperate.

"If you need me, I'll be here," she says to the nurse as she checks her phone. "Going to wait for the social worker. Thought she'd be here by now."

Rising, I follow the girls and the nurse down a stark white corridor and into the third door on the right. The exam room is close quarters, but we all manage to fit.

"I'm Becca." The nurse removes the silver stethoscope from her neck and smiles a careful smile at Wren. "Would you mind having a seat for me on the table? I just want to listen to your heart and get a quick blood pressure on you."

The girls don't speak, don't move.

"It's okay," I tell them, my voice a gentle push. "Nobody here will hurt you."

The nurse glances at me before turning back to them and offering a nervous smile. I imagine she was briefed before we got here, but nothing could've prepared her for seeing these two in the flesh.

"I'll go first," Wren says to her sister, climbing onto the end of the table. The crumple of thin paper beneath her fills the small room along with the trace of musky, unwashed hair.

The nurse places her metal bell against the back of Wren's chest, instructing her to take two deep breaths, and then she places the blood pressure cuff around her arm, explaining every step of the way. When she's finished, she has Wren step on a scale so she can get her height and weight. Becca scribbles the numbers on her clipboard before setting it aside and turning her attention toward Sage.

Glancing at the paper, I spot *#95* and *62 inches* scribbled in blue pen.

Underweight. As if we needed a scale and a ruler to confirm that.

"Sage, are you ready?" Becca asks, replacing the paper on the exam table with a clean pull. Sage hesitates before obliging, and the process is repeated.

A quiet knock on the door precedes the entrance of a white-haired doctor with dark pink lips, striking hazel irises, and clunky silver earrings. She moves to the sink first, washing her hands with an overdone thoroughness before turning to offer the girls a grandmother-like smile.

"I'm Dr. Halifax," she says. "You can call me Dr. Corinne if you'd like."

It takes a second for me to realize another woman is standing behind her. With dark circles under her kind, hazel eyes and bushy brown hair that suggests she skipped a shower to come straight here, she wears exhaustion like a second skin, but the laminated badge hanging from her neck identifies her as Sharon Grable, LISW. The hospital must have assigned them a social worker.

Dr. Corinne grabs the nurse's paperwork and takes a seat on a rolling stool, scooting closer to the girls, and Sharon leans against the wall, keeping out of the way.

"This is Sharon," Dr. Corinne says, pointing behind her. "She's here to help you."

The social worker steps forward. "We're all here to help you. Whatever happened . . . whatever you've been through, I want you to know you're safe here, and we're going to see to it that you have somewhere safe to go."

"Our sister," Wren says, her voice cracking from too much silence. "Her name is Evie. Is she here?"

"Deputy May mentioned you were looking for your mother and your sister," Sharon says. "We're going to do everything in our power to find them, but we need to take things one step at a time. As soon as Dr. Corinne is finished, the police are going to ask you some questions—questions that could help us find them. But if at any time you're feeling overwhelmed or you need to take a break, you let us know, okay?"

The girls nod, and Sharon moves back to the wall, her off-white sweater fading into the cream-colored walls.

"So I understand you two were in the woods," the doctor says, crossing her legs and running her hand along the stethoscope that hangs over her shoulders. She smiles, the lines beside her pretty eyes crinkling. "Can you tell me what you were doing there?"

The room is hushed as we wait for a response. Over the years, there have been all kinds of stories, mostly local lore, about the Stillwater Forest and the kinds of people who may or may not reside somewhere deep inside. It seemed like most residents laughed at the stories, but some took them so seriously they wouldn't step foot beyond the hiking trails and the little rusty children's park beside the seldom-used campground.

Brant says it all started after someone's baby was taken from that park, and the rumors grew from there.

Wren clears her throat, her shoulders almost slouched and her posture less intense, which I hope is a good sign.

"We had to leave our home," she says, swallowing, her eyes dancing between Sharon and the doctor. "Mama took Evie to town because she was sick. Then a man came. And he wouldn't leave. He was going to take us, so we waited until he was sleeping, and we left."

The doctor tries her best to keep an unfazed expression, but the veins in her neck pulse, and she has to look away.

"How long have you lived in the woods?" Dr. Corinne asks once she's gathered herself again.

"When can we leave?" Wren ignores the doctor's question. "We need to find our family."

Sharon takes a step away from the wall, her palm raised. "Girls, more than likely you'll be kept here tonight for observation. You'll see another doctor, and there'll be some tests. They just need to make sure you're healthy before they can release you."

Wren slides down from the table. "No."

She reaches for Sage, whose dark brows are angled inward, and takes her by the hand.

"You said you would help us, but you're forcing us to stay here." Wren's words are rushed as she pulls her sister to the door.

Dr. Corinne rises, but Sharon places a gentle grip on the doctor's shoulders.

A moment later the girls run out the exam room door, disappearing down the hall. Up until now, it was easy to lose myself in the moment, to become a fly on the wall, a passive observer quietly trying to wrap my head around how this could've happened.

But I can't let them get away.

They won't survive out there on their own.

They need someone. Someone like me. Someone they can trust.

Then again, if they survived in the wilderness, maybe I'm not giving them enough credit.

"Wren, Sage," I call as I trail behind them. "Please, wait."

The girls squeeze between nurses and crash carts and portable computer stations and stop when they reach a door at the end of a hall that can only be accessed with a bar-coded badge. When they turn to face me, they're breathless, with eyes like frightened, wild animals that've been cornered.

I keep my distance, placing my palms up. "It's okay. I *promise* you're safe here."

Wren's face is pinched, like she doubts me. "You said we'd be safe. You didn't say we'd be kept here against our will."

Pulling in a deep breath, I nod. I can't begin to relate to how they're feeling, but I can understand it, respect it.

"I know this is confusing to you," I say, "but you need to trust that these people have your best interests in mind. They want to make sure you're healthy and that you're feeling well enough to answer the questions the police are going to ask so they can find your family. And once we get through that, they'll find you a place to stay."

"A place to stay?" Sage asks.

"It's not like we can go home. He'll find us there. And he'll probably kill us after what we did," Wren adds.

My heart gallops as I try to piece this together. "If someone wants to hurt you, he won't hurt you if you're here. There are guards here. And doctors and nurses. Locks on every door. Cameras."

It sounds like I'm describing a prison, though I'm not even sure if these girls know what that is if they've never left the confines of their little house in the woods until now.

The girls' silence almost makes me lose hope, but then Wren whispers into Sage's ear before turning to me.

"Only one night?" Wren asks.

"Yes. And then we're going to find you a place to stay," I say, hoping I'm not overstepping my boundaries. I don't know what the exact protocol is here.

"Where?" Wren asks.

"There are foster homes . . . places that volunteer to take in young people who need help," I say. "How old are you?"

"I'm nineteen," Wren says. "Sage is eighteen."

I begin to say something, but I stop myself from expressing an ounce of disbelief at their ages. I thought they were young teenagers at the most, maybe fourteen or fifteen. I didn't know they were adults.

Wincing, I massage my lips together, contemplating whether or not I should say something. It isn't my job to let them know that they're too old to be placed in a foster home . . . and even if the state makes an exception for Sage, more than likely they'll be separated, and Wren will be on her own. With no help or resources, there's a chance she would wind up in a homeless shelter somewhere.

"Everything okay?"

I turn to find Sharon standing halfway down the hall, just past the exam room.

"You ready to go back?" I ask the girls.

They take each other's hand and start walking back, and I follow, a wild hair of an idea filling my mind.

I'm going to take them in.

Then they won't have to be separated; they won't have to meet yet another stranger or spend night after night sleeping on cots in youth and women's shelters. After the trauma they've been through and the uphill battle they're facing, this is the best solution for them. I wouldn't be able to sleep at night if I turned my back on them.

I'm happy to open my home to these sweet girls even if the timing isn't exactly convenient given the current questionable state of my marriage.

Heading back into the room, I make a mental note to call Brant about this later. I can't imagine he'll be upset with me for doing the right thing.

And if he is?

It's the least of my concerns.

CHAPTER 23

Wren

"Here you go." Nicolette appears in the doorway of the room she's just put us in, an armful of clothes and extra blankets in her arms. My sister has hardly moved from the edge of the large bed that sticks out from the wall by the giant window. Nicolette offered to give us each our own room with our own private bathroom, but I insisted that we stay together.

I haven't told Sage this, but I'm just as scared as she is.

There's a book Mama used to read to us when we were little. These kids walked through the back of this wardrobe and into this whole other land with all these mythical creatures and things and people they'd never seen before.

That's what this is like, only this is real life, and there are no mythical creatures—only dozens of faces I've never seen, introducing themselves with names I'll never remember and spouting out titles I've never heard of as if it makes them more trustworthy.

I don't know whom to trust, whom to believe. Who's good and who's bad. And if Mama could lie to us, then so could anyone else.

"Thank you." I take the clothes from Nicolette and set them on top of a dresser. Earlier today, she brought clothes to the hospital for us to come home in. They're too big on us, but they're soft and they smell nice. Someone with Deputy May took our dresses and coats and placed them in a clear bag. I don't know if we'll ever see those clothes again, but I think I'm okay with that because I've yet to see a single person dressed like we were.

"Tomorrow," Nicolette says, "if you're feeling up to it, maybe we could go into town? Get you both some new clothes?"

I swallow. "All right."

"Do you want me to show you around the bathroom?" she asks, eyeing the doorway between our bedroom and the small room connected to it. "There's a soaking tub in there and some bubble bath under the sink that smells like spearmint and eucalyptus. Might feel good to soak for a bit. I imagine you're still sore."

I don't know what "bubble bath" is, but it sounds nice.

Her eyes drop to my bare feet, which still ache and are marred with red marks and blisters from our journey two nights ago.

"Here. I'll show you." Nicolette walks into the bathroom, and I follow. "So you turn this knob to here for warm water. Turning it to the left will make it hotter, right will make it colder—kind of like the shower at the hospital." Plucking a pink bottle from under the sink, she unscrews the cap. "You pour one or two capfuls of this under running water to make bubbles. When you're done with your bath, there are robes and towels in the closet here. Press that silver button on the tub to drain the water."

"Thank you." I stand in the doorway between the bedroom and bathroom as she shows me how to operate the large, oval-shaped basin against the wall. From the corner of my eye, I see that my sister still has yet to move. "I've never had a . . . bubble bath . . . before."

Nicolette's lips curl softly. "Well then, you're in for a treat."

Our baths were much different from this. Twice a week, Mama would bring in a small copper tub and fill it with well water that she would heat over the fire. We'd take turns, but the water was either too hot or too cold, and we were prompted to get out before we had time to get comfortable. Days between, we'd wash with soap and a washcloth.

I'll take a bath . . . but not tonight.

Nicolette says they have a security system here and that even if the man found us, he wouldn't be able to get to us.

I want to be with my sister right now. She's the only thing that feels like home.

"If you need anything, I'm next door," she says. "Just knock."

She gives us a warm smile before leaving, and I'm not sure if I'm supposed to close the door behind her or not. Everyone around here seems so big on doors and privacy, treating every room like their own personal space. I'm not sure if I could ever get used to that.

Crawling into bed in the "sweatshirt" and "leggings" Nicolette gave me, I slide under the covers.

"You going to go to sleep?" I ask Sage, who hasn't moved from the edge of the bed since we got here tonight.

Turning toward me, she inhales a quivering breath. "Why did Mama lie to us?"

"I don't know." My voice fades in my throat. "I'm too tired to think about that right now."

I lie to my sister, but it's for her own protection. She doesn't want to know even half of the thoughts that have crossed my mind in the past twenty-four hours. One minute I'm angry, the next I'm confused. But mostly I'm in disbelief, hoping and praying we'll see Mama soon so she can explain.

Mama loves us. But she lied to us. That's the only thing I'm sure of.

"You think we'll find them?" she asks.

"I don't know."

"Do you think the man will track us here?"

"I don't know, Sage," I say, tugging the covers up to my neck and staring at the ceiling at some kind of circular light with five flat blades sticking out like spokes in a wheel. I'll have to ask Nicolette what that does in the morning. "Just . . . come to bed, okay? We'll talk about this tomorrow. Get some rest. We're safe here."

For now.

I think.

I hope . . .

CHAPTER 24

Nicolette

I lower the volume on the TV so the girls don't hear what the locals are saying about them. TV was a concept they'd only heard of once before yesterday, when they came face-to-face with one in their shared hospital room, and I'm not sure they'd even understand the concept of gossip or late-breaking news stories, but one less reminder of their current situation is . . . one less reminder.

"They're calling them the Stillwater Darlings." The youthful, raven-haired news anchor with a voice beyond her years stares into the camera, shoulders straight and brows holding just enough concern. "Early yesterday morning, two teenage girls wandered out of the Stillwater Forest looking for family they say abandoned them in a cabin in the woods. Authorities are still trying to piece together this disturbing case, but they're saying there is very little information to go off of. No photographs. No birth records. No addresses. Not even a last name. We'll be bringing you the Stillwater County Sheriff Department's press conference in just a moment, but for now, we ask that anyone with any information related to this case, please contact the following number."

The screen turns blue, and a local number flashes across, bold and white. A moment later, the camera pans to an empty podium. The rustle of paper and clicking of cameras and low hum of voices chattering in the background come to a stop when a gray-mustached sheriff approaches the stand and adjusts the microphone.

"As many of you have heard, yesterday at approximately 0700 hours, two young women . . ." He gives his statement, providing the press with a formal report containing nothing that I didn't already know. "The department is currently searching for a woman with blonde hair and blue eyes, average height and build, late thirties to early forties, as well as a young girl with blonde hair, approximately nine years old. We believe this woman and child to be the family of these girls. If you have any information, please call the sheriff's department immediately. I'll now open the floor to questions."

He points to a journalist off camera, whose question I can't hear.

"No comment on that at this time," he answers.

Heading to the en suite, I take the opportunity to wash up for the night, borrowing Brant's artisanal face soap in hopes that the lavender chamomile scent might help me fall asleep easier tonight.

I need to call him again. So far all my attempts have been feeble.

It isn't unusual for him to be out of reach when he travels. Not everywhere he goes has adequate cell tower coverage, but going more than a day or two without talking together is rare.

Climbing into bed, I pull my phone from the charger and try him one more time—this time opting to call the hotel phone directly—before I crash for the night.

"Hello?" He answers on the third ring, catching me off guard.

"Everything okay?" I ask.

"Yeah, of course. Why wouldn't it be?" He laughs at my question.

"I've been trying to reach you since yesterday."

"Unfortunately cell towers in the Amazon are few and far between," he says with a chuckle. The sound of rustling sheets fills the earpiece, and I imagine him settling into his hotel room after a day of shooting, a crystal tumbler of hotel bourbon resting on a coaster beside him, the TV muted in the background, English subtitles flashing across the screen.

He was using the hotel's WiFi when we FaceTimed the other day. Was he not at the hotel yesterday?

"That's what I figured," I say, wondering if he picks up on the curtness in my words, the reservation in my tone. "I've taken in two young women."

Silence.

"Wait," he says. "What?"

"Their names are Sage and Wren. They're eighteen and nineteen."

More silence, silence that feels ironically loud somehow, but his speechlessness doesn't frustrate me. This would come as a shock to anyone.

"I thought . . . don't I have to be there to sign something?" he asks. "We haven't even done our home study."

"We're not fostering them," I say. "They're going to be staying with us until we can reunite them with their family."

"Nic . . ." His voice dwindles into nothing for a moment. "This is . . . wow . . . I don't know what to say here."

"You don't have to say anything. It's an unfortunate situation, and I just want to help them any way I can," I say. "Maybe check the channel four news website when you get a chance."

He agreed to the fostering thing. In my opinion, this isn't any different.

"It's been a long couple of days," I say. "I'm exhausted."

He draws in a long breath, saying nothing, though I can only imagine what he wants to say in this moment.

"I'm sorry," he says. "I know this isn't the reaction you were hoping for. It's just . . . it's going to be an adjustment, that's all. I'll get used to it. We'll make it work."

"As opposed to not making it work?"

"You know what I mean." His tone is sharp, sharper than mine.

I can't help but wonder if this complicates things for him.

And I can only hope it does.

CHAPTER 25

WREN

I wash my hands in the bathroom with a bar of milky-white soap, and I breathe in a comforting lavender scent that reminds me of home.

I don't know how anyone can live with all these windows.

Our cabin had four windows, and at times that almost seemed too much. If we needed more light, we went outside. The only time the windows were appreciated was in the winter, when the sun happened to be shining and we wanted to pretend the threat of frostbite didn't linger in the air.

Nicolette gave us what she called "the grand tour" this morning before breakfast, and I'm not sure she has a single room in this entire house without a window or "skylight" in it—most of them bare and uncovered. She says she likes natural light and that out here the woods give them plenty of privacy, but then she stopped herself, saying, "or the illusion of privacy, I suppose."

Sage and I take our seats at her kitchen table as she moves around the kitchen in a pale robe covered in a lilac print, her thick, crimson hair tied in a smooth-as-glass bun on the very top of her head.

I've never seen hair so sleek and glossy.

My sister rests her elbow on the table and her chin in her hand, watching Nicolette using all these little machines and electrical gadgets to whip up our meal.

Electricity is a strange concept.

I flip a switch. There's light.

I press a button. My food is piping hot.

There's even a machine that keeps food cold on one side and freezing cold on the other. Nicolette says food lasts much longer that way because she can control the temperature—unlike our root cellar.

"Would you like some help?" Sage offers, rising with slow intention.

Nicolette pauses, holding what appears to be a loaf of sliced bread wrapped in clear shiny film with the words "100% whole wheat" in bold green letters along the side.

"Only if you'd like to, sweetheart," Nicolette says.

"She's good in the kitchen," I say. Though I'm not sure how good she'd be in a kitchen like this . . .

Sage tries to temper her excitement before bolting up from the chair and heading across the room.

"Do you have a spare apron?" she asks.

Nicolette reaches into a drawer to the left of the sink, retrieving a red gingham smock much like the one we had back home. I wince, fully expecting Sage to lose her merriment at the sight, but instead, she grabs it, tying it around her waist without giving it a thought.

I should've given her more credit. Sage has always been more resilient than I.

"Had you ever seen a toaster before?" Nicolette asks, sliding the shiny, rectangular box across her white countertops. Sage shakes her head, and Nicolette proceeds to explain how to make the warm, crunchy bread.

In a matter of minutes, breakfast is done, and the smells that fill the kitchen make my stomach rumble. Nicolette places our food on clean white plates with sprigs of parsley on the side. She said not to eat the parsley—that it's only for looks, but I don't know why someone would waste a perfectly good herb. If anything, I'll use it as a breath freshener.

"How would you girls feel about going into town today?" Nicolette asks, pushing her plate away and reaching for her coffee. "We could get you both some new clothes. There are a couple of shops I think you'd like."

She lifts her mug, examining us like she does. Part of me thinks we're just as fascinating to her as she is to us. Everything about her is sweet and soft, and she smells like soap and flowers. I can't help but feel we're weeds in this beautiful garden of hers, but she doesn't treat us that way.

"May I be excused?" I ask when I'm finished.

Nicolette takes a sip, brows lifted. "Of course."

I carry my dish to the sink, eyeing a bottle of blue liquid marked "dish soap" alongside a yellow sponge. Twisting the faucet knob, I rinse my plate under the water, nearly scalding my hand when the water that spits out is burning hot. My elbow brushes against Nicolette, who's suddenly standing behind me, and I jerk away.

"You don't have to do that," she says with a smile before pointing to a silver machine built into her cabinets. She reaches toward it, yanking open the door. "This is a dishwasher. We put our dirty dishes in here, pour some soap in the little container, then press this green button and shut the door. A few hours later . . . clean dishes."

She slides the lower rack out and shows me where the plate goes. My hand still throbs from the hot water.

Convenience is wonderful until it isn't.

"I should get ready," I say, backing away.

Heading upstairs, I pass an image on the wall of Nicolette in an ivory gown, a man standing behind her dressed in black and white, his arms around her as he grins ear to ear. She mentioned she's married and that her husband's name is Brant and that we'll meet him soon—as long as we're ready—but she hadn't shown me his picture.

There's something familiar about him, something I can't quite place. Glancing toward the kitchen, I hear Sage and Nicolette chatting and the clink of silverware, and I turn back to study Brant's face once more.

Pulling in a sharp breath, I hold it, letting it burn in my chest as the realization comes to me.

It's his eyes . . .

They're the exact shade of sea-green as Evie's.

CHAPTER 26

Nicolette

"Thank you so much for doing this," I say over the phone to Dr. Pettigrew, the psychiatrist who evaluated the girls at the hospital their first night. "I feel better knowing you're there in case anything upsets them. And I could use someone, you know, in case the media shows up. They've been leaving us alone so far, but you just never know."

"It's really no problem," she says. "It's my day for rounds at the hospital, but I got someone to cover me for the morning, so it worked out. I just can't stop thinking about those girls. I'll help any way I can."

The girls are dressed in various items pulled from my closet, all of which hang off their lanky frames. I thought about buying new clothes for them myself, but I haven't the slightest idea what sizes they wear. The clothes they were wearing when they showed up were handmade. No size tags for obvious reasons. A short and protected shopping excursion seemed like the best way to handle this. Besides, it might be good for them to get out and interact with people who aren't medical professionals or police officers. To get the smallest sample of true freedom. I can't imagine forcing them to stay cooped up and hidden away in my house after they just escaped from a similar situation.

"We should be at the boutique in about an hour," I say as I pad into the next room, passing the stairs and glancing up. The girls are supposed to be getting ready, but the house is so quiet I can hardly tell they're here.

I expected teenagers to be louder.

But these two aren't typical teenagers in the slightest. They're simply little humans, suspended in their own reality.

"I'll see you soon," Dr. Pettigrew says before hanging up. When I get a chance today, I'm going to have to talk to her about how best to introduce the girls to Brant. They seem to be fearful of men, and from what I understand, they'd never seen one until that man broke into their home and held them captive.

Why a man would randomly come across their home—a home that no one knew existed—and proceed to hold them captive for a number of days using nothing but threats . . .

He didn't hurt them. Didn't abuse or assault them sexually or otherwise. But he was going to take them somewhere . . .

Even the local police are scratching their heads, which isn't to say a lot because landing a case like this hasn't happened in the hundred-and-fifty-year history of the department, but still . . .

A large man with dark hair and marks on his face would stick out like a sore thumb in a town with a population of two thousand, and yet no one around here has ever seen or heard of anyone remotely fitting that description.

The other day, Deputy May briefly mentioned looking into a couple of missing-children cold cases from years ago, saying they were trying to match up ages and descriptions, but she said it could be a lengthy process. Besides, Wren's age doesn't appear to fit either of the profiles. And while Sage claims to be a teenager, her appearance is closer to that of a twelve-year-old.

Heading upstairs to check on the girls, I knock on the guest room door, which is already open.

"Girls?" I call when there's no answer.

"In here," Wren says from the bathroom.

"We should get going soon. Dr. Pettigrew is going to meet us there." I check my watch.

Glancing toward Sage, I watch as she brushes her teeth in front of the mirror, my clothes hanging off her tiny frame and her dark hair sopping wet, soaking the collar of her shirt. It's thirty degrees out—I can't let her go outside like this.

"Sage, would you mind if I braided your hair?" I offer. "It would look so pretty in a French braid . . . then we could get it off your shoulders. It's a little chilly outside . . . I'd hate for you to get sick."

She places her toothbrush back in the holder before meeting my gaze in the mirror's reflection, and then she nods.

"Wren, I can braid your hair, too, if you'd like?" I offer. I don't wait for her to respond before I head to my room, returning with hair ties and a can of aerosol hair spray.

Fifteen minutes later, I've braided their hair and led them down to the shoe closet, pulling out tennis shoes that are two sizes too big for each of them, but they're the only thing that will work because at least we can tie the laces tight enough to hold them on.

Grabbing my keys off the console by the back door, I jingle them in my hands. The girls are surprisingly not as nervous as I expected them to be. This will only be the second time they've ventured into town in their lives, and they've never set foot in a shop or store.

It's a peculiar sight, these two in their baggy clothes and sopping-wet braids and still hollowed-out expressions. There's a little more color and life in their complexions than there was a couple of days ago, but they still remind me of abandoned baby bunnies, always together, always with a cagey glint in their shiny eyes.

"Shall we?" I ask, pointing toward the garage entrance. The two follow me, sneakers shuffling against the hardwood floors. When we get to the car, I grab the doors for them. "Don't forget your seat belts."

I watch as they tug and pull their restraints into place and wait for the satisfying click that ensures they're safely buckled.

Climbing into the driver's seat a moment later, I start the engine, glancing into the rearview mirror, where Wren is seated, staring toward Brant's parked Tesla beside us.

"You'll be meeting my husband soon," I tell her, realizing he comes home in two days. "But only if you're ready."

The chime of my phone fills the car speakers while Brant's name flashes on the control center screen.

Speak of the devil.

I press the button on the dash to transfer the call from Bluetooth to my device so he's not on speakerphone, and I put in an earbud.

"Hey," I answer as I back out of the driveway.

"Nic," he says, voice groggy as if he just woke up. "How's, uh . . . how's everything going?"

"Great. Better than expected, actually."

"Listen. I'm sorry about last night," he says, exhaling. I'm not surprised he's apologizing. Brant hates conflict—or at least the Brant I know does. "I was a little blindsided. To say the least."

How does it feel, Brant?

"Understandable." I pull onto the highway, headed into town, going easy on the gas. On the way home from the hospital yesterday, I noticed they tensed up and grabbed each other's hand anytime the car went above thirty miles per hour or hit a pothole.

"I saw the articles," he says, "about the girls."

"Yeah?"

"And I think it's incredible that you're taking them in," he says. "I don't know that a lot of people would take that on."

I bite my tongue, keeping myself from telling him that they're not feral children. As far as anyone can tell, they're just two young women who grew up isolated from the modern world. Growing up in the wilderness doesn't make them wild any more than standing in a garage makes me a car.

"Anyway, I'm coming home a day early," he says, "to help you."

I haven't yet told him about the girls being wary of men, and I was hoping to buy some extra time to prepare them, maybe tell them more about him, show them photos and videos.

"You really don't have to—"

"Nic, it's already done. I'm leaving first thing in the morning. Should be home by dinner tomorrow night."

In the distance, I spot rumble strips and a stop sign. I need to give the girls a heads-up.

"Can I call you later?" I ask.

"Of course."

I end the call and point over the dash. "The car is going to vibrate in a few seconds. It's nothing to worry about, okay?"

As I press my foot into the brake, we slow to a stop, the car vibrating over the ridges in the road. When I glance into the rearview mirror, the girls don't seem the least bit fazed. Exhaling, I flick on my right turn signal and silently scold myself for not giving them enough credit.

I don't know much about them yet and I don't know what all they've endured, but I do know they're irrepressible little things, fighters in every sense of the word.

A minute later, I'm pulling into a parking spot outside the Jade Boutique on Hancock Drive. Dr. Pettigrew is seated on a painted park bench outside the Victorian house-turned-shop, and she smiles when she sees us.

"Wren, Sage, you remember Dr. Pettigrew," I say as we climb out.

"It's so nice to see you again," the doctor says, tugging her pearl-buttoned cardigan down around her pencil-thin hips. "I've spoken to one of the sales associates inside. She's got a fitting room set up for us, and she's already pulled a few items."

Getting two teenage girls complete wardrobes from a privately owned boutique isn't going to be cheap, but I don't think these two are exactly mall-ready yet. There's a Walmart fifteen miles away over in Pearson Township, but even that might be overwhelming with its abundance of fluorescent lighting and never-ending maze of aisles.

Climbing the steps to the front door, I spot a handwritten sign that reads, Closed For Private Shopping Event, just as I'd requested.

Jade Boutique is ready for us. Soft music plays from speakers in the ceiling, and the faint scent of gardenia wafts from a candle centered on a marble-topped console beside a navy velvet settee. Three dressing rooms with white satin curtains for doors flank the left wall, and a cash register resting upon a jewelry display case flanks the right.

There isn't much to pick from here, and I don't think teens are Jade's targeted demographic judging by all the florals, but I have no doubt we can find them enough to get by. And if I can figure out their sizes, I can order a few more things online when we get home.

"Hi there, how are you?" A young woman with a sleek onyx braid down her back, honey-toned skin, and bright fuchsia lipstick struts toward the girls, extending her right hand. "I'm Monica. I'll be helping you today."

I've shopped here a handful of times before, mostly out of boredom since this place isn't exactly my style, and never once has Monica greeted me with a handshake. I was worried the locals might give the girls the same cold shoulder they gave me, but maybe I was projecting? Maybe they'll be embraced with open arms?

The girls glance at her extended hand for an awkward second before Monica quickly retreats. I'm sure Dr. Pettigrew briefed her before we got here, and I'm sure as a Stillwater local, she's seen and heard all about these girls, but it's impossible to know which words and concepts and behaviors are foreign and which are familiar to them.

"If you'd like to follow me," Monica says, turning on her beige Chanel flats, which I'm 99 percent sure are replicas. No one in Stillwater would spend a thousand dollars on shoes no matter how fashion conscious they claim to be. "I've pulled a few things for you and hung them in your rooms. If you want to get started, we can see where we're at size-wise and go from there. Sound good?"

Her voice is high-pitched, and her manicured hands clasp together. I'm not sure if she had way too much coffee this morning or if she's overcompensating with the friendliness because these two make her nervous; either way, it doesn't seem to faze the girls, who head straight into their dressing rooms and begin staring at all the clothes on hangers and hooks.

Wren traces her hand over the fabric of a navy gingham dress before inspecting the seams.

"Everything all right?" Dr. Pettigrew asks. "If you don't like that style, we can find you something else."

Wren's pink lips curl. "It's beautiful."

Collectively, we release our held breaths, and Monica steps toward them, fussing with the ties on the dressing room curtains.

"Go ahead," Monica says. "Try it on."

I take a seat on the settee next to the doctor, and we wait forever before Wren emerges from behind the drapes, the blue gingham dress fitting her reedy frame perfectly, even giving the illusion of a girlish figure in parts.

"So?" I rise. "What do you think?"

With glassy eyes, she bites her lower lip before whispering, "I love it."

Sage emerges from her room next, a pair of skinny jeans hanging off her and a button-down top that might look better on someone two or three times her age.

Tugging on her pants, Sage wrinkles her nose. "I don't like these. They make me walk funny."

Wren laughs. Then Sage. Spritely giggles fill the small shop.

It almost makes it easy to forget that the forest that surrounds our quaint little town is filled with police, search dogs, and volunteers, all combing through the thick trees and rough terrain in search of bodies dead or alive.

I've never seen such little spirits lifted so high, and it sends a squeeze to my chest. In this moment, I wholeheartedly believe everything's going to be okay.

Monica prompts them to try on the next outfit, and they disappear behind the curtains once more. Grabbing my phone from my purse, I fire off a quick text to my hairstylist to see if she can fit the girls in for haircuts today.

A moment later, I clear my throat, leaning closer to Dr. Pettigrew. "My husband's coming home tomorrow . . . He's been gone for work, and they haven't met him yet."

The doctor turns her focus on me.

"They freaked out when they saw those male cops that morning," I add. "And they made sure there were no male doctors or nurses treating them in the hospital."

"That was a precaution," Dr. Pettigrew says. "I don't think they're afraid of men so much as they're afraid of the man who held them captive in their home. They'll be fine. You're a kind woman to take them in. I imagine your husband is just as kind as you are."

Placing my palm over my beating heart, I offer a close-lipped smile. Her words both comfort and sadden me all at once.

Once upon a time, Brant was the kind of man who'd help stranded motorists and nurse baby birds back to health. He once stayed up all night long baking me a three-layer chocolate cake from a recipe he coerced out of my favorite New York bakeshop after the local bakery screwed up his order and we had company coming to town the next day for my birthday.

He used to fix my coffee for me after my postrun shower, and he'd treat me to fresh flowers every time he went into town. Always roses. Always white.

Once a year, he'd surprise me with a romantic getaway. I always knew it was coming, but I never knew when or where we were going.

He'd simply wake me up on a random morning and tell me to pack my bag.

Recalling all the sweet things Brant used to do for me does nothing but paint a vivid picture of a hard truth: the man I'm married to isn't the man I married.

And as soon as he comes home, I need to get back to finding out exactly who he is.

The last couple of days have provided a temporary and much-appreciated distraction from my personal chaos, but reality, much like a scorned ex-lover, will not be ignored.

CHAPTER 27

Wren

"Cut it off," I tell the pretty lady as she drapes a black smock around my chest and shoulders and ties it behind my neck. It's loud in here. And bright. And it smells like a hundred different kinds of those essential oils Mama would line her dresser with. Bottles upon bottles, all with paper labels and Mama's handwriting. Tuberose. Gardenia. Pink pepper. Eucalyptus. Lemongrass. Orange blossom. "All of it."

Our eyes catch in the mirror, and the woman runs her fingers through the wavelike bends from the French braid Nicolette placed in my wet hair this morning.

"Are you sure?" she asks, biting her lip before looking to Nicolette, who's standing off to the side with my sister. "You have such beautiful—"

"I'm sure." I sit taller, straighter, chin pointed as I stare at my reflection.

Mama let us cut our hair about once a year, and even then, she never allowed it to be above the middle of our backs.

"My darlings, long hair suits you better," she would say, snipping at our fraying ends and every so often repositioning our heads. *"It only accentuates your natural beauty."*

The more I'm around Nicolette, the more I see how controlling Mama was all these years. We never had any kind of a say in what we wore, what we ate, what time we went to bed, or how we kept our hair.

But with Nicolette, every decision is only ours.

There's freedom in the way she lives. She's not bound to anyone or anything. There are no silly rules. No irrational logic. No need to question anything. If she wants to do something, she does it, and that's all there is to it.

If Mama were here, I'd ask her why she wouldn't cut our hair. I can't imagine it had much to do with protecting us from the evils she claimed lurked in a place that has, so far, treated us with nothing but kindness.

"Why don't we take it to here?" The lady with the comb places her flattened palm at my shoulders. "Then you could still wear it up if you wanted?"

"That will be fine," I say.

The woman leads me back to a chair attached to a washbasin, and she tells me she's going to "shampoo" me. A moment later, a stream of warm water rains down my scalp, followed by the subtle scent of flowers as her fingertips massage my scalp.

It's almost how Mama used to do it, only Mama was never this gentle, and the water was always cold by the time she got to me. She'd always use the warm water on the younger ones, saying they needed it more than I did.

The woman wraps a towel around my head and leads me back to her chair, taking her time combing it out before the first snip is made. I squeeze my eyes shut at first, though I'm not sure why, and by the time I open them, I'm surrounded in the kind of lightness I've never known.

Sage hasn't looked up from the booklet Nicolette gave her, carefully selecting her hairstyle. As the woman rubs lotions throughout my damp strands that smell nothing like the coconut salve Mama used on us, I can't help but think about Evie. Where she is. What she's doing. If Mama's filling her head with the same old lies.

And that's exactly what they were.

Lies.

Our entire *life* was a lie, and if it wasn't? Then nothing around me makes sense.

Mama's stories aren't adding up.

On the way here, I saw people walking dogs, unbothered by the cold and waving to one another with gloved hands and colorful knit scarves and hats. They seemed happy to be outside, happy to see one another, smiling and exchanging "hellos." I also saw houses beside houses, shops beside shops, cars parked all along the sidewalks. When Mama would talk about her childhood, she'd mention those things, but she'd talk like they weren't around anymore, that the world was a sick and twisted place and there was nothing left but the ruins of a beautiful place that once was and never would be again.

The lady grabs a small black machine and clicks a button on the side. In an instant, a burst of hot air blows hair into my face. After a few minutes, my eyelids become like weights on my face. I could fall asleep right here in this chair. Everything feels so good, and I don't know why.

"What do you think about this one, Wren?" Sage taps my shoulder, shoving the booklet at me and pointing to a photo of a girl with blunt hair just past her shoulders and fringe along her forehead that stops at her eyebrows.

"I think that would look lovely on you," the lady says over the loud hum of her machine. "Excellent choice."

Tonight I'm going to take one of those bubble baths Nicolette was telling us about last night. And I might even borrow one of the books from her library. I pulled a few fiction novels earlier today, before we left for the clothing store. I couldn't stop staring at their vivid covers and breathing in the clean scent of their crisp, ivory pages. They weren't musky with spines so cracked you could hardly read the lettering. They were little works of art, and there were *hundreds* of them all lined up neatly in a bookcase as wide as her wall, spanning from the floor to the ceiling.

I'm going to read them all.

The woman clicks the machine off, and the blanket of heat that surrounded me is quickly replaced with cool air. She reaches for another piece of equipment, this one long and slender, and she begins running it over the length of my hair, section by section, letting each strand return to my shoulders with a gentle fall.

From beneath the apron that covers my shoulders, I lift a hand to my hair, gliding my palm over my silken locks. With all this shine, my hair looks more golden than ever, and I can't stop studying my reflection.

I do that a lot now . . . now that there are mirrors everywhere I go.

That's another thing—people love their mirrors here. They're in bathrooms and bedrooms. Hallways and cars. Some women even carry them in their bags everywhere they go. We only ever had one, and we hung it above the washbasin. Mama mostly used it when she was doing her hair, but for the most part we had no use for it.

I always knew what I looked like, but it wasn't something I concerned myself with or thought about too often. But the last couple of days, every time I pass a mirror, I can't help but stop and stare, studying my features and still wondering why I don't have a single one in common with Mama.

I picture my bright-yellow hair next to her wavy, dark-blonde locks. My hooded eyelids next to her prominent dusky blue gaze. Mama had a strong jawline, a "German jaw" as she always called it, and everything from her brow line to her chin was defined, chiseled almost. My face is quite round in shape, my features all soft and smooth compared to hers.

I never told Mama, but every once in a while in those "false memories" as she called them, there was a woman. A woman who wasn't my mama but looked at me like she was. She had the same saffron-gold hair as I do, though hers was curly, and when she smiled there was a gap between her front teeth.

I've seen that woman in my dreams so many times I could probably sketch her from memory.

"Nicolette?" I ask.

"Yes, sweetheart?"

"Do you think we could order some paper and pencils from your supply man?"

Her mouth rises at the sides. "Of course. Actually, there's a place down the street that sells them. We'll stop there as soon as we leave."

Tonight I'm going to try.

CHAPTER 28

NICOLETTE

"How did you meet him?" Sage asks as she flips through a photo album and studies an image of my husband.

Brant should be home any minute, and I can't stop looking at the clock. I spent the afternoon on the phone with Dr. Pettigrew, quietly hashing out various scenarios and how to handle them, though she assured me the girls are adjusting well—better than expected—and she didn't anticipate any issues. Nevertheless, she rattled off a bunch of signs to look for, signs that the girls are uncomfortable but not necessarily vocalizing it. I scribbled them down and shoved them in my pocket, though I'm not sure why. I've read them enough today that they're burned into my memory.

"I worked at an art gallery," I say, taking a seat on the floor next to the coffee table. "He was a photographer—up and coming at the time—and he came in to ask my boss if he'd feature his work . . . which was pretty gutsy, especially in New York. But he was good, and he was tired of waiting around to be discovered. Anyway, I'm rambling. He came into the gallery, met with my boss, and when he came out of that meeting, he asked me for my phone number, and we met later that week for drinks."

All this time, I've been worried about how the girls are going to react when they meet him, when really I should be worrying about how they might feel if they like him—as everyone always does—and I end up kicking him out.

I'd hate for them to hand over their trust to a seemingly good man, only to learn that he's a liar and a cheat. I'm not sure how traumatic that would be for them given the fact that their first experience around an adult man was less than ideal.

I remind myself to take things one step at a time, to cross these bridges as they come.

"What does that mean—meet for drinks?" Wren asks, slicing through one of Brant's old dress shirts with a pair of heavy sewing shears. This morning over breakfast, she insisted on sewing Sage a new doll to replace the one they had to leave behind. She says she's going to sew one for Evie, too, to give to her when she sees her again.

"It's when two grown-ups go to a bar and drink grown-up drinks—alcohol—and get to know each other," I say, watching intently as she licks the end of a thread and points it through the head of a needle.

She's going to sew it all by hand, every last stitch.

"What's alcohol?" Sage asks.

"It's a drink that makes you feel funny," I say, drawing my knees against my chest as I settle in for girl talk. "Like . . . relaxed. But it can also make you do things you might not otherwise do, so you have to be extremely careful."

Sage flicks to the next page in the album, running her palm along the glossy pages and tracing Brant's face.

"He's pretty," she says.

"Handsome," I correct her with a forgiving half smile. "And yes, he is."

Wren pokes the needle through two pieces of Brant's shirt and glances up. "How long have you been with him?"

"A long time," I say. "Years. Married ten. Together thirteen. Something like that."

"Why don't you have kids?" she asks.

My response catches in my throat. No one's ever had to ask me that before because everyone in my little circle has always known about my hysterectomy.

"We wanted to," I say, speaking slowly. "About ten years ago, I had a medical emergency. After that, I wasn't able to have children."

Saying it out loud after all these years doesn't make it sting any less than it did a decade ago.

"Anyway," I say, clapping my palms on my thighs and smiling through the tears that threaten to come, "they say everything happens for a reason."

"Who says that?" Sage asks.

"It's an expression," I say.

Sage turns to a new page, feasting her dark eyes on a selfie of Brant and myself in front of the pyramid of Giza several autumns ago. Her small fingertips trace the lines on his face. "He looks like a nice person, Nicolette."

Wren looks at me before she meets Sage's gaze, and her expression is blank, unreadable. While I have nothing but admiration for that brave little soul, I'm finding it a bit hard to connect. She rarely speaks unless she has to, but she always looks like she has something to say; I'm hopeful that with time, she'll be able to open up to me.

Rising, I head to the kitchen to grab a glass of water, stopping in my tracks when I see two xenon headlights pointed through the front windows. The metallic clunk of a car trunk slamming follows next.

He's home.

CHAPTER 29

Wren

Nicolette wrings her hands as she stares toward the front door. Glancing out the windows that frame the entrance, I spot the outline of a dark figure pulling something behind them. The sun went down hours ago, so it's hard to make out any details, but for a fraction of a second, my muscles seize, convinced it's the stranger coming back for us.

"Brant's home," Nicolette says, but I don't believe the excitement in her tone because her eyes winced and she hasn't moved an inch.

The door swings open a second later, and a man comes into view. He looks exactly like his photos, maybe better. Sandy-blond hair with a slight wave, a square jawline with full, blush-colored lips, and piercing yet soft green eyes just like Evie's.

He's tall but not nearly as tall as the stranger who broke into our cabin. And even with his black woolen jacket, I can tell he's strong but not in a monstrous sort of way. Nothing about him seems threatening, and his smile seals the deal.

Still, I keep myself at a safe distance. I don't know him, but I want to like him because I want to stay here.

I like it here.

Everything's warm and soft and pretty and nice . . . and safe.

"You must be Wren?" Brant asks, releasing the handle of his bag. Shrugging out of his jacket, he folds it over his arm. He doesn't come toward me, doesn't extend his hand toward me like the sales associate did at the boutique. He keeps back. "Brant. Nice to meet you."

Sage appears behind Nicolette, her dark eyes studying the handsome husband of the gracious woman who took us in.

"And you must be Sage?" he asks. He has dimples. Like Evie.

"You have a good trip?" Nicolette asks as he steps toward her. Brant places one hand on her arm and leans in, kissing her cheek. Her body tenses as he touches her.

"Good but long," he says. "Just wanted to get home. I've missed you."

He pulls away, and their eyes meet, holding like they're having a conversation without so much as saying a single word.

"Should I make some tea?" Nicolette asks, her question directed to us. "Maybe we could chat for a little while before you girls head to bed?"

Sage yawns, and I catch one myself.

Nicolette turns to her husband. "It is a little late for them . . . maybe they can get to know you better in the morning?"

"Of course," he says, eyes smiling as he gazes at me, then to my sister. "It's a date."

Slipping my hand in Sage's, I lead her upstairs to our room, and then I close the door. She peels out of her clothes and into a pair of pin-striped pajamas Nicolette bought her at the boutique yesterday, and then she crawls into her side of the bed.

I'm not tired, but I don't want to be down there, with them, marinating in a tension so thick I could slice it with a butter knife.

"He seems nice," Sage says, rolling away and keeping her back to me as I change.

"Yeah."

"They make a lovely couple. Like a prince and princess."

I tug my shirt over my head and fold it neatly on the dresser before slipping out of my skirt.

"They do," I say.

A moment later, my sister's breathing has softened and steadied. Reaching for the book on my night table, I pad toward the window seat and draw the curtain until I have enough moonlight to read the words on the pages.

Ten chapters later, I'm reading the author's biography, and while my body is heavy and leaden, my mind is whizzing and whirring. I couldn't shut it off if I tried.

Drawing in a deep breath, I place the finished book aside and tiptoe across the room, quietly twisting the doorknob and ambling downstairs to grab my sketch pad from the kitchen table, where I left it earlier today.

I was trying to draw the woods, at least the woods the way the Gideons see them. Needled pines mixed with bare stalks of trees. Wild turkeys. The occasional deer. It's like looking at my home but from a stranger's perspective. Everything's the same, and yet everything's different.

I make it downstairs and find my charcoal pencil and sketchbook right where I left them. Heading back to my room, I stop when I reach the top of the stairs and hear Nicolette and her husband's rushed, muffled voices.

"Why are you acting like this?" she asks.

"I'm worried this is going to make things worse," he says. "For you."

It feels wrong to eavesdrop, so I creep back to my room and shut the door, heart pulsing in my ears and tiny, quick breaths escaping my lungs.

I knew there was something going on between them. I saw it in her eyes. In his, too.

My stomach is clenched, knotted tight. Her husband doesn't want us here. I haven't the slightest idea where we would go from here. Without Nicolette's charity, who knows what would become of us?

Maybe if I'm nicer to him, he won't feel this way? And that could buy us more time to find Mama and Evie?

Giving myself a moment to settle down, I crawl into the window seat once more and draw my knees up, resting the sketch pad on top of my thighs. A moment later, I drag my pencil against the cream-colored, paper. Drawing has always calmed me, much like the way reading does.

Closing my eyes for a second, I picture the lady with the curly yellow hair and the gapped smile. I've never drawn her before because I never wanted to upset Mama, but tonight I'm going to. I'm going to bring her to life right here on this paper.

Painted in moonlight, I sketch the outline of her face first—round like mine—and then her nose, small and buttonlike. I give her a wide smile and pale, bushy curls that frame her face. Every time I close my eyes to picture another one of her details, there's a weight on my chest, a fullness, and a tingle that spreads all the way to my toes.

I don't know what it means, but I can't help feeling as though I know her.

CHAPTER 30

Nicolette

"What's this really about, Nic?" Brant asks, tugging his navy cashmere sweater over his head.

I slip my wedding ring from my finger and place it in the heart-shaped box on my nightstand.

"Taking in the girls . . . staying in New York for the winter," he continues. "There's something deeper going on here."

"Just admit you don't want them here," I say, keeping my voice low yet tight in my chest. I don't want the girls to hear any of this because no matter what's said tonight, it won't change anything. I'd sooner kick my husband out than put those poor girls on the street with nothing and no one. "Stop trying to pick fights about me when this is really about something else."

He scoffs. "Something else? Nic, this is about *you*."

"Me?" I chuckle. Talk about deflecting.

I read an article online last week about cheaters, and they all do the same thing when they're trying not to get caught: deflect, distract, deny.

"You want to know what I think? I think you're in over your head here. You're taking on too much," he says, working his belt buckle and shoving his jeans down his muscled, runner's legs. I steal a peek of his rippled abs, the ones that haven't grown an ounce of body fat in the thirteen years we've been together, which is more than most husbands can say. It's funny how we stop appreciating these little things the more we're around them, like we've seen them so much, we're physically incapable of seeing them anymore.

Brant would be heart-stopping eye candy to any other woman, and I know that.

"You know how you get this time of year, and when you add something like this on top of it," he says, "I worry it'll take a toll on you."

"It won't."

"And if it does?" He lifts a single brow.

I slide beneath the covers on my side of our massive bed, twisting to fluff the pillow behind me. I'm not even going to dignify his question with a response because this entire conversation is pointless and not worth a freckle-size speck of my energy.

Exhaling, he takes a seat beside me on the bed, his body bare save for his navy-blue boxer briefs. In the pale moonlight, his eyes glint, and the soft, natural scent of his warm skin fills my lungs.

If this were before, I'd be lying in his arms right now, feeling the burn of his lips against my flesh as his fingers tug and pull at my garments, exploring the parts of my body that have always belonged to him and only him.

Those days are gone, though. And even if we were to somehow get back to that . . . it wouldn't be the same.

It will *never* be the same.

Brant reaches for my hand, holding it in his and running the pad of his thumb along the underside of mine, and I allow it, reminding myself he doesn't know that I know anything, and I need to keep it that way.

But there's nothing inside me when he touches me, no flutter in my middle, no thrum in my chest.

We might as well be rooted islands separated by an ocean.

"I just . . . I wish you'd have asked me first," he says.

"You'd have said no."

"I wouldn't have," he says. "I agreed to do the fostering thing with you, and I know this isn't really different . . . but we have to be a team. We have to make these decisions together. We need to be on the same team here."

My eyes find his in the dark. I'm not sure what this pep talk is about, but last I knew, when you're on the same team, you don't run off and have a baby with someone from the opposing side.

Pulling my hand from his because I don't have what it takes to fake this bullshit heart-to-heart a second longer, I slide my back against my pillow, sinking down into the mattress.

"I'm tired," I say. "And it's late."

"I know, I know." Brant sighs. "We'll start fresh tomorrow."

He strides around to his side of the bed before climbing in next to me. A moment later, his hand wraps around my waist, and he pulls me against him, burying his head in my neck, breathing me in the way he did when he once loved me and only me.

Eyes shut tight, I will myself to sleep, begging my mind to silence long enough that I can drift off without issue, but all I'm met with is the soft rumble of Brant's breath in my ear and his warmth on my skin. He's out cold, sleeping like a proverbial baby, my body half-pinned beneath his weight.

I can't breathe, so I fling his arm off me and slide off the mattress. He rolls to the other side, stirring for a few seconds but never waking, and his raspy, steady breathing continues.

Running my hands through my hair before gathering it over one shoulder, I watch my husband sleep, jealous of his ability to shut out the rest of the world when mine is screaming in my ear every time I see him.

Deciding to go downstairs, I shut the door behind me and take soft, creeping steps as the rest of the house sleeps. A second later, I'm cozied in an oversize leather chair in the living room, a knit blanket wrapped around me as I stare through the picture windows toward the moonlight-painted woods behind our house.

Flashes of light in the distance serve as a reminder that the police are still searching for the girls' mother and sister. They haven't stopped. Combing the woods could take weeks, they said. There's a lot of ground to cover, and they're not going to stop until they've searched every square inch.

Resting my chin against my hand, I stare at the yellow speck of flashlight in the distance, trying to wrap my mind around what kind of woman would hide her kids away from the rest of the world.

Was she a selfish monster?

Or was she simply a woman willing to do whatever it took to keep her babies safe?

I won't let myself judge her. I don't know the full story. No one does. Perhaps they were escaping an abusive husband who wanted to hurt them . . . or worse?

Whatever it is, I'm sure she had a compelling reason.

No one would have done what she did without one.

The yellow flash grows closer, pointed down at times and swaying at others. I rise from my chair, the blanket wrapped over my shoulders as I approach the window to get a closer look. Only the light disappears by the time I get there.

All I see now is darkness and the outline of trees, tall and spindly, fading to black in the distance.

That can't have been a searcher . . .

They wouldn't be alone in the woods at midnight.

And they certainly wouldn't kill their light.

The light by the road flicks on—the city has it on some kind of energy-saving system, and I've yet to figure out its schedule in nearly ten years of living here. I shuffle toward the windows by the front door and manage to make out the outline of a person at the edge of our long driveway, standing perfectly still.

An object is clutched in his right hand—a flashlight, I presume—and there's something hanging off his back—a bag?

His light clicks on a second later, and he points it at our garage.

Heat creeps up my neck, stopping at my ears, turning my face numb in the places my blood runs cold.

The figure moves closer, toward the house, but I don't wait to see what he does next. Sprinting upstairs, I fling our bedroom door open and begin to shake my husband at the shoulders.

"Someone's here," I whisper once his eyes half open.

His arm lifts as I startle him out of his deep sleep, and he reaches for the lamp at his bedside table, but I stop him.

"There's a man," I say. "Outside. In our driveway."

He sits up, more alert now, and I reach for my phone.

"I'm calling the police," I say, dialing 911 with trembling fingers. "Don't wake the girls."

Brant flings the covers off his legs and grabs a pair of plaid pajama bottoms from a drawer, stepping into them and tying the drawstring around the waist before finding a clean white T-shirt.

Heading into his closet, he emerges a moment later, his handgun clutched at his side, and then he disappears into the hallway.

"Can you make sure there are no sirens?" I ask the dispatcher after explaining our emergency. "I have two girls here . . . I don't want to wake them."

"We typically don't use sirens this time of night unless we have to, but I'll make sure the officer knows," she says.

When I finish the call, hands still shaking, Brant stands in the bedroom doorway.

"He's gone," he says. "I checked the security cameras. There's no one out there. He must have left."

Pressing my hand against my chest, I collapse on the foot of the bed. "I just thought . . . I didn't know if it was the man . . . the one the girls say might be looking for them."

"You did the right thing," he says, dragging his hand through his thick, sandy-colored hair. "I'll go downstairs and wait for the police. You should get some sleep, Nic."

Brant lingers, studying me, and the tone of his voice holds a mix of exhaustion and condescension.

He doesn't believe me.

A moment later, the door closes, and I'm alone in our room, sentenced to bed like a child.

I know what I saw.

I know someone was out there.

CHAPTER 31

Wren

My neck throbs, forcing me awake, and my lower back pops when I shift.

I fell asleep in the window seat last night.

Glancing down, I spot a blanket over my legs and my sketch pad on the floor. The bed is made, pillows fluffed, and covers pulled taut.

Sage must be downstairs already.

Heading to the bathroom, I wash up for breakfast before trekking downstairs. Brant and Nicolette's whispered words play in my mind when I see them sitting across from one another at the kitchen table. Her slender fingers wrap around a white coffee mug, and his muscled shoulders fill out a white T-shirt as he laughs at something Sage said. When I look closer, I realize he's showing her some black device that fits between his hands. Nicolette said he's a photographer, so I imagine that's his camera.

For someone who doesn't want us here, it's sure hard to tell.

He must be good at lying. Like Mama. He must be able to say things with such conviction and do things with such intention it makes it hard for anyone to deny them.

Still, I promised myself I'd make an effort . . . for Sage's sake. For mine, too.

"Good morning," I say, forcing a smile.

"Good morning, Wren." Nicolette's face lights, and she shoves her chair out from the table. "Hungry?"

"Nic makes the best blueberry waffles from scratch," Brant says. "You have to try one."

Ambling toward the stove where Nicolette prepares my plate with waffles, scrambled eggs flecked with dill, and thick, peppered bacon, I thank her before helping myself to a glass of orange juice and taking a seat at the table.

"Wren is an artist, too," Sage says to Brant. The two of them look to me, and Brant lifts his brows.

"Oh, yeah? What's your medium?" he asks.

"My what?"

"What do you use to create your art?" he clarifies.

"Oh, I draw," I say. "Pencil and paper."

"She's really good," Sage says, nibbling on a piece of crunchy bread.

"You have anything I can see?" he asks.

I think about the drawing of the lady with the yellow hair upstairs, but I don't want to have to explain it. I'm not sure there's anything I can say about it that won't make me seem troubled or delusional.

"I'm working on something," I say, "but it isn't ready yet."

"Has Nic shown you my studio yet?" he asks.

I shake my head. She took us past it the other day but told us it was the only part of the house that was off-limits because it was where Brant did his "edits" and he liked to have everything just so.

"You should check it out after breakfast," he says. "Lots of natural light, plenty of desk space. I could set you up with a little corner so you can sketch in there anytime you want."

Nicolette's gaze moves to his.

"That would be wonderful," I say. And I mean it. I appreciate that he's sharing his special place with me because it means he's trying . . . and it means he might open up to the idea of us being here.

Brant begins to reply, only he's interrupted by someone pounding three times on the front door. His smile vanishes, and Nicolette drops the green kitchen cloth in her hands. The two of them exchange looks and, without saying a word, make their way to the foyer.

When I glance outside the window above the kitchen sink, I spot a police car parked in the driveway, like the one Deputy May drove us to the hospital in that first day.

"Stay here, girls," Brant says before disappearing into the next room.

Sage's dark eyes lock on to mine, but I have no words of comfort or reassurance to offer myself, let alone her.

Taking the chair beside her that still holds Brant's warmth, I slip my hand over hers.

Whatever happens, we'll always have each other.

CHAPTER 32

NICOLETTE

I shrug into my winter coat and step outside to meet Deputy May under the cover of our front stoop. A moment later, Brant joins me. The gray sky is bright, blinding my tired eyes, but I manage to squint enough to focus on May's face.

She isn't smiling.

"Where are the girls?" she asks.

"Inside." I point behind me. "Why? What's going on?"

"We found a woman's body in the woods," May says, a deep line forming between her brows. "She matches the description the girls gave of their mother . . . at least from what we can tell. She's been there a while."

"Oh, God." I pull in a breath of cool, wintry air destined to turn to clouds, my feet frozen to the cement steps.

"Identifying the body could be traumatic for the girls," May says, "so we're hoping to compare her DNA to the samples we took of the girls at the hospital. The lab's going to prioritize the testing, but it could still take up to seventy-two hours at the soonest. Sometimes longer."

"We're better off not telling them then," Brant says, hands resting on his narrow hips.

"Right," May says. "But I at least wanted you two to know, so you're not blindsided right along with them in a few days."

Despite not having definitive proof of the woman's identity, my heart breaks for Wren and Sage already. If it is her, it means their mother is dead. If it isn't, it means their mother is still missing, and we're not any closer to finding her.

"And the little girl?" I ask. "No sign of her?"

The deputy shakes her head, adjusting her hat. "We're still searching. Next department over loaned out their tactical chopper, and we were able to locate the cabin the girls were living in. From there, we collected a few things that we should be able to send off for DNA testing. You never know if someone's in the system already. A lot of times that's why they're living in hiding like that."

Deputy May reaches into the right breast pocket of her uniform, pulling out a pen and a small spiral-bound notepad. A moment later, she scribbles her number and hands it over.

"I don't give this out," she says. "Ever. But I want you to call me anytime day or night if you need anything."

"Thank you," I say, folding the paper between my fingers.

"First watch said they were called out here overnight, possible trespasser," she says, eyes moving between Brant and myself.

"Nic thought she saw someone standing at the end of our driveway," Brant says, exhaling.

"I *did* see someone," I say. "He had a flashlight. And a bag on his back. He came out of the woods."

"You were also tired, and it was pitch-black outside. For all we know, it could've been a deer or something," he says, placing his hand on my shoulder and giving it a squeeze. He doesn't give me a chance to so much as mention the streetlight by the road before he says, "Anyway, thanks for coming out here, Deputy. Appreciate you personally delivering the news."

May rests her hands on her duty belt, directing her attention to me. "How are they doing?"

"Wonderfully," I say. "They're brave and resilient and curious. You wouldn't know they've just been through something so awful."

"It's incredible, isn't it? How resilient the younger ones are," she says.

"It really is." I nod.

"What about you?" she asks. "How are you holding up with all of this?"

My head cocks, and I struggle to find an answer, but only because I'm not sure why she felt the need to ask this question or how it's any of her concern. "I should get back inside. Thanks for this. I'll call you if anything comes up."

Holding up the creased slip of paper, I offer a quick smile, and we watch May return to her car.

"What do we tell them when they want to know why she was here?" I ask Brant.

He drags his palm against his bristled jaw, staring hard at the ground, lost in thought. "We'll just tell them that they stopped by to let us know they're still searching and that they located their cabin."

"That woman in the woods . . . do you think it's their mother?" I ask.

His eyes hold mine, and a chill breeze kisses my face.

"I don't know, Nic," he says. "All I know is it's dangerous to assume things, especially when those assumptions turn out to be wrong."

CHAPTER 33

Wren

The natural light flooding Brant's studio the next afternoon warms my skin as I take in the sights beyond the glass. Before, it was simply a closed-off room behind a locked door, and I didn't concern myself with what was behind it. Now I've been granted an all-access pass by Brant himself.

Three walls are nothing but windows, offering a panoramic view of a hilly portion of the forest, and it faces east, so the sunrise fills the room with warmth in the morning. I didn't much care for the windows before, but this beautiful view makes me forget the dangers that lurk beyond the trees.

Three guitars rest on stands next to a leather chair in one corner, and beside them is what Brant called his "music setup." I've never seen anyone play a musical instrument before. He said he'd play for me sometime.

Before he finished showing me around yesterday, he gave me one of his old "cell phones" and taught me how to listen to songs on it—any song in the world. When he asked me who my favorite artist was, I just shrugged, so he took the device out of my hand and told me he'd make me a playlist.

The only wall in here that isn't covered in windows is covered in the most beautiful pictures, and Brant was sure to tell me there's nothing wrong with taking pride in your work. He also says he'll tell me about his "humble beginnings" one of these days.

It was the first time I'd really thought about Brant and Nicolette and who they were before. Where they came from. What their families were like.

Brant says everyone has a past. *Everyone.*

Earlier today, he ran into town for a couple of hours, and when he came back, he handed me a package of watercolor pencils and three small paintbrushes, with red, yellow, and blue handles.

It's *really* hard not to like him.

I crumple a piece of sketch paper between my hands and toss it into a chicken-wire wastebasket. The music player next to me plays a song called "Pink Moon." I can't help but think of warm summer nights when I hear it. As soon as it finishes, I press the left arrow button to play it again, just how Brant showed me.

Mama got us a ukulele one year for Christmas, but Sage broke a string on it before anyone had a chance to learn to play it properly. No one seemed all that upset, and we never bothered to fix it after that. Music in our home was usually just me and Mama trying to harmonize and Sage warbling along with us while Evie plugged her ears.

But this . . . I could get used to.

Flipping to a fresh page in my sketchbook, I get to work. This time I'm drawing Evie—partly because I miss her and partly because I want Nicolette to give this to Deputy May. Maybe it could help them find her?

A half hour later, I set my pencils aside and massage my cramped hand before stretching my arms above my head. I straighten my spine and feel the relief of each pop and crack of my back. Pressing the square button on the phone, I silence the music. I've probably listened to "Pink Moon" about a dozen times now.

Holding up the image of Evie, I blink away the warm wetness that clouds my vision. I've colored in her creamy complexion, her rosy cheeks, and her green eyes, but now I need to grab a cup of water so I can use the paintbrush to soften the strokes and blend it together.

Rising from the stool, I turn to leave, nearly bumping into Brant. He reaches for my arm, steadying me so I don't fall, and then he laughs.

"Sorry," he says with a slight chuckle. "Didn't mean to scare you."

His eyes skirt past my shoulder, landing on the notebook and the image of my sister.

His smile vanishes, and then he swallows. "Who is that, Wren?"

"Evie," I say. "My other sister."

Pallor washes over his face but only for a second. And just like that, his color returns.

Clearing his throat, he mumbles something about needing to find his thirty-millimeter lens, and a moment later, he's gone.

CHAPTER 34

Nicolette

"You can have any one you want," I say. "Just know the ones with the boring boxes are healthier, and the ones with the bright colors are full of sugar."

The girls say nothing, staring with wide eyes down the cereal aisle at the Stillwater Grocery Mart.

We've been here for over an hour already, our excursion taking a little longer than usual because the girls are processing everything, accepting samples, asking questions, and reading packages to find out what's inside.

I told them they could have anything they wanted. They've been deprived their entire lives, so I figured this was the least I could do, but so far the only things they've placed in the shopping cart are vegetables and oats and then cooking staples like molasses and brown sugar.

"Is this one good?" Sage holds up a box of cinnamon-and-sugar squares. The tag in the corner claims there are twenty-eight grams of whole grains and nineteen essential vitamins and minerals in each serving.

You only live once . . .

"It is," I say with a smile. "Wren, you find one you like?"

She reaches for a blue box with an orange tiger on the front, clutching it against her chest as she carries it to the cart.

Glancing at my watch, I tell them, "We should head to the checkout now."

The girls follow, keeping close behind me, and we pick a lane that doesn't have a wait but does have all the candy in the universe wrapped into one strategically crafted display case.

"Go ahead," I say, pointing.

Wren shakes her head. "No, thank you."

Sage grabs a box of grape Nerds, shaking it, and then grabs a package of Sour Skittles and a Mars bar.

"Nicolette?" Wren asks when we're almost finished.

"Yes?" I answer, digging through my wallet for my debit card.

"I drew some sketches of Mama and Evie . . . do you think the police would want to take a look at them?"

I know the girls gave them the physical descriptions of their mother and sister that first day, but I don't believe they've sat down with a sketch artist yet.

"Of course. Everything helps."

She releases a harbored breath, smiling, and it breaks my heart that she felt the need to ask for permission. I can't help but wonder how much of her life was under someone else's thumb . . . and I'm beginning to think the answer is: all of it.

"How are you liking the studio?" I ask. It's a miracle Brant opened that space to her. He rarely lets me set foot in there, but he seemed to have rolled out the red carpet for Wren.

And it's funny, because I expected Wren to be hesitant with him, to be leery, but if anything, he's brought out a warmth in her that wasn't there before. I see it in her eyes, in her willingness to join in conversations instead of sitting back and being a fly on the wall.

"I love it," she says, though her jovial expression fades as she leans in. "Nicolette?"

"Yes?"

"I heard you two fighting the other night." Her eyes rest on mine.

My cheeks burn. "Oh . . . um . . . I'm so sorry . . . you know . . . marriage is a lot of work sometimes, and we don't always see eye to eye. I'm sorry you had to hear that."

"He doesn't want us here, does he?" she asks.

"God, no," I say, wishing we were in a place where I could wrap her in my arms and hug her until she could feel the sincerity in my tone. "I don't want you to ever worry about that. Ever."

Wren's mouth twitches into a hint of a smile, and she nods. "Okay."

"It'll be two hundred eight dollars and ninety-four cents," the woman running the cash register says. I insert my card into the chip reader, punching in my PIN as I feel the weight of her stare in our direction. "Hey, aren't you girls those Stillwater Darlings? They find your family yet? Heard they found a body in the woods."

She clucks her tongue, hunched over her lane and lending a sympathetic gaze. I'm sure she means well, but she has no idea what kind of fire she might have just ignited.

"That forest always creeped me out," she says, shuddering as if she's shaking off a spine-tingling chill. "Heard there were crazies living out there. Baby snatchers."

The cash register door opens and shuts, and the woman yanks my receipt from the printer, handing it over.

"Got to love small-town lore." I offer a polite smile.

The cashier peers over her nose at me, like she's offended I'm brushing off her ridiculous nonsense.

"Thank you," I say, refusing to answer her questions or engage in her rumor-fueled commentary. "Come on, girls."

We load up in record time—many hands make light work. And when we're finished, the girls climb in back and sit side by side behind me. Sage on the left, Wren on the right.

"Nicolette?" Sage asks once we merge onto the highway.

"Yes?" I meet her stare in the rearview mirror.

"Why did that lady call us the Stillwater Darlings?"

"It's just some silly name some local news station came up with," I say. "News agencies, they're really in the business of selling ad space—advertisements—so they need these sensational stories and sensational headlines. But you know what? It's a good thing in this case because the more people who hear about you, the more likely someone might come forward. Somebody somewhere knows something."

The girls are quiet for a moment, and I tighten my fingers around the steering wheel while I wait for the inevitable next question.

"Why did she say they found a body in the woods?" Sage asks, her voice low and barely audible over the road noise.

Clearing my throat, I pull in a deep breath. This isn't how I wanted to tell them or when I wanted to tell them—I was going to wait until we got home so I could sit them down, but it seems the choice has been made for me already.

"The police did find a body," I say. "But they haven't identified it yet. They'll tell us as soon as they know something, I promise."

We drive three miles before anyone speaks again.

"When do you think they'll know if it's Mama or Evie?" Wren asks. There's a strain in her voice, her tone deflated.

"Sweetheart, I'll tell you as soon as I hear something. I promise."

Slowing as I approach my turn, I glance back for a second only to spot their skinny little fingers laced together. Wren stares out the window. The remaining ride home is silent, save for the low-volume drone of the seventies rock station playing on the satellite radio.

As soon as we pull into the driveway, I back into the garage and pop the trunk. Brant's car is gone; his side of the garage is vacant. And only when the girls and I are carrying bags in do I remember the area code 212 phone calls on Fridays between nine and ten in the morning.

"Why don't you two go relax for a bit?" I ask, hoping they don't sense the distraction in my tone.

Sage plops down at the kitchen table, her three packages of candy displayed before her like prized treasures. Wren disappears around the corner, the tromp of her footsteps going upstairs and dissipating into nothing, only to return a moment later.

"Nicolette," she says, breathless and eyes wide.

"What is it?" I place the gallon of skim milk in my hand on the counter. "Wren, what's wrong?"

"My drawings," she says. "I left them in Brant's studio. They're gone. The ones in my room, too. They're all . . . gone."

CHAPTER 35

Wren

He took them.

I know he did.

But why? What could Brant possibly want with sketches of Evie and Mama?

"Where do you think he is?" I ask Nicolette, who's standing next to the counter.

"I don't know, sweetheart. Maybe he went for a run?" She folds a paper bag and places it aside.

She lifts a container of milk off the counter and slides it onto a shelf in the refrigerator, her back to me. Maybe she doesn't think this is a big deal, but it's a big deal to me—especially after the way he looked at my drawing of Evie earlier and then left as if nothing had happened.

"When do you think he'll be back?" I ask.

Nicolette shuts the refrigerator door, her hand lingering on the handle and her back still toward me. "He's never gone very long. I'm sure any minute now."

Her answer doesn't quiet my mind the way I wish it would.

"Are you sure you didn't misplace them?" Nicolette reaches for another bag, retrieving items and arranging them on the counter. "Not saying I don't believe you, but I don't know why Brant would take something from your room, something so . . . personal."

I watch Sage, who's in her own little world, ripping through colorful packages and shoving candied bits into her trap like they're going to disappear if she doesn't eat them fast enough. It reminds me of the way she is with snow candy.

"We'll ask him when he gets back," Nicolette says when she turns and realizes I haven't moved an inch. "I'm sure he's got a perfectly good explanation."

Something in her tone doesn't let me believe her.

I don't think I can trust him.

I don't think he's one of the good ones.

CHAPTER 36

Nicolette

Perched on the edge of the bed in one of our spare rooms, I glance out the window that overlooks the driveway from the second floor, my phone pressed against my ear as I wait on hold with our cell carrier. I need to see when Brant gets back.

It's been easy to let the girls become a distraction from the issues at hand, but when Wren came to me a short while ago saying Brant took some drawings from her room, I tried my best to pretend it wasn't a big deal, that I was sure there was a logical explanation, but the truth eluded me.

That isn't something Brant would do—not the Brant I know.

"Hi, yes," I say when a customer service rep finally comes on the line. "I'm needing to check and see what the last five outgoing calls were on one of our lines."

The woman on the other end is silent at first, maybe judging me, but I don't care.

"The passcode on the account?" she asks.

"Gideon777," I say.

"And which line were you wanting to know about?"

"The one ending in three-five-six-two," I say, my palm clutching the phone.

"All right. You have a pen and paper handy?"

"Ready," I say, reaching for the leather-bound day planner and pen that I'd tucked under my arm on the way upstairs.

"Most recent one is two-one-two . . ." she says, rattling off that same New York number that littered last month's phone statement. The lady spouts off the rest, all of them occurring last night, and none of them being suspect.

"Thank you," I say, hanging up in the middle of her asking me if I'd answer a five-question survey once we disconnect.

He called her.

He called her while I was in town with the girls.

I toss the phone on the bed and stare at the number. Dragging my hands through my hair, I pace the room, swallowing gulps of air and trying to figure out how I'm going to bring this up and when and what's going to happen when I do.

Taking a seat on the bed again, I reach for my phone, attempting to steady it in my shaking hand as I accept that there's only one thing I can do here.

I have to call her.

Clearly, freezing the account and dropping hints that I know about the "fraudulent" activity has done nothing to deter him from sneaking around behind my back, so it's come to this.

Pressing *67 first, I dial her number and hold my breath.

Four rings later, I'm met with a greeting: "You've reached Beth. Leave a message."

Beth . . .

Is that who my husband fathered a daughter with?

Striding across the room, I fling the door open and march toward our master suite. Digging into his sock drawer, I reach to the very back, beneath the organizer tray and the silky black dress socks he rarely wears . . . only there's nothing.

I pull everything out, lining it up haphazardly on the dresser top until the entire drawer is vacant—and that's exactly what it is. Vacant.

The photo of the girl is gone.

My stomach bubbles, and bile burns my throat. Running to the bathroom, I kneel at the toilet, dry heaving until my middle is in knots and my lungs are gasping for air.

I need to stop digging and prying and delaying the inevitable all in the name of finding stone-cold evidence. How much more proof do I need? What am I waiting for? Evidence that I'm wrong? That this is all a bad dream?

There's a reason he's been pilfering my money away, hiding this girl from me, and speaking to a woman named Beth every Friday morning while I'm gone.

And I'm going to find out—from the source himself.

With a single wretch, I lose the contents of my stomach. My dignity and my pride follow as I wipe the burning bile from the corners of my mouth with a wad of toilet paper.

So this is how it ends.

We won't end up pleasantly plump, white-haired retirees spoiled by a tropical climate.

We'll end up going our separate ways, him running back to New York to be with the little family he created when I was none the wiser and me starting over, alone, emotionally devastated.

The beep of the alarm chime on the front door tells me he's back. Hurrying to our bedroom, I shove his socks back into place and ensure they're as neat and aligned as they were before I ransacked the drawer.

A moment later, I give myself a once-over in the dresser mirror, smooth my hair into place, and head downstairs to finally face the truth.

CHAPTER 37

Wren

Lying on the sofa in what Nicolette calls "the family room," I page through one of her paperback books. In this one, a woman exacts revenge on her husband for cheating on her; she fakes her own "kid-napping" and death and tries to frame him for it.

My fingers tingle as I devour each page, unable to read it fast enough.

I've never read anything so clever and sharp, and I'd never known the concept of "kidnapping" until I found it between these pages.

This is exactly the kind of book Mama would've burned in the hearth, but as long as I'm reading, as long as I'm lost between these pages, I don't have to think about the body they found in the woods.

While my eyes scan the next page, I find myself wondering if Mama would've done something like this Amy character.

I decided earlier today that my memories about the house with the soft floors that tickled my feet and the flower walls—the ones Mama said were false—were real. And if I squeeze my eyes tight enough and concentrate, I can almost hear the shrill ring of a yellow phone hanging on a wall in a kitchen. It made the same sound Brant's iPhone makes when someone calls him.

The house in my recollections had compartments, rooms with doors—like Nicolette's, only smaller. It wasn't one giant room like our cabin. And I had my own room, with pink curtains and a white bed with something over the top of it. Some kind of fabric maybe? I'm not sure what it was, but it made me feel safe and protected.

How could I envision something like that if I'd never seen it before?

It had to have been real.

There's no other explanation.

Just thinking about it sends a tightness to my chest and a fullness throughout the rest of my body—unlike anything I've ever felt before.

I don't even know what it means. I just know it's real, and Mama's not here anymore to tell me that it isn't.

Returning to my book, I flip to the next page only to hear the sound of Brant's voice.

He's home.

I place my book on the little table beside the sofa and leave the family room, finding him in the hallway hanging up his jacket in a closet.

"What did you do with my sketches?" I ask my burning question.

Turning toward me, he winks. "Ah. Was hoping you wouldn't notice."

And then he smiles all the way from his mouth to his eyes. I don't.

"Where are they?" I ask.

"I was hoping to surprise you," he says, stepping toward me, arms out and palms up. "Took them into town to get them framed. Should be ready by Monday."

"Why?" My fingers drum against my sides.

"*Why?* Are you serious? Wren, your drawings are incredible. I don't think you realize how talented you are. Your work deserves to be archived and showcased."

Cocking my head and squinting, I study him.

"How'd you know about the ones in my room?" I ask. As far as I know, he hasn't stepped foot in the guest room I share with my sister.

He laughs through his nose, hands on his hips. "I was walking by. Door was open. Saw them lying there on the dresser . . . I'm sorry. If I'd have known this would upset you, I never would've done it."

"What's going on?" Nicolette stands at the bottom of the stairs, her dark-blue gaze passing between the two of us as her hand grips the railing. Her face is paler than usual, her hair out of place in some parts.

Brant turns to his wife. "I took her drawings into town to get them framed at the frame shop. Was trying to do something special . . . you know, artist to artist."

She studies him, though I can't tell if she believes him or not.

Turning back to me, he says, "Look. You can go into town with me to pick them up if you want."

Exhaling, I let my arms fall to my side. If he was trying to do something special for me, then I'm being rude. After all, he did tell me not to be shy about showcasing my work.

I suppose after everything that's come to light recently, it's easy for me to cast doubt.

"I'm sorry," I say, not wanting to cause trouble. "I overreacted. I get attached to my art, that's all."

"You and me both. Don't even worry about it." Brant swats his hand through the air before resting it at his hip. "Completely understand."

Heading back to the family room, I leave the two of them at the bottom of the stairs by the coat closet, and I lose myself between the pages of a book where nothing is truly as it seems and no one is who they claim to be.

Thank goodness it's fiction.

CHAPTER 38

Nicolette

If things were different, our weekend would be filled with things like me teaching the girls how to order pizza and how to play classic games like YAHTZEE, Monopoly, and Sorry! I'd teach them the marvels of a washer and dryer and introduce them to the last two decades' worth of pop music. Somewhere along the line, we'd squeeze in a half dozen Disney movies while we paint each other's nails and page through fashion magazines.

If things were different, I could give them back their childhood and adolescence, as much of it as possible and in as little time as possible because any day now, we're going to find out about that body in the woods, and their young little lives could use a little less tragedy.

But instead, I'm standing face-to-face with my philandering husband.

"Hey," he says, shoving his phone in his pocket.

Scanning the length of his jeans-and-polo outfit, I ask, "No run this morning?"

He shrugs. "Rest day."

Folding my arms along my chest, I ask, "What are your plans now?"

He glances toward the stairs. "Just going to get some work done."

My husband smiles before passing me and climbing the stairs. A moment later, I watch as he pulls his phone from his jeans, checking it quickly before sliding it back into his pocket.

The entire time I've known him, he's always had to work in "airplane mode." No internet, no WiFi, no phone calls.

No exceptions.

"Expecting an important call?" I ask.

He scoffs. "What?"

"You're taking your phone to your studio."

As he turns to face me completely, I catch the subtle flare of his nostrils. "Yes, actually. I *am* expecting a call."

My skin is on fire and the room begins to spin, but I have to do this.

"From Beth? In New York?" I ask. "Oh, wait. You only talk to her on Friday mornings between nine and ten. While I'm not around. That's right . . ."

"Nic . . ."

I don't want to fight in earshot of the girls so I climb the stairs, pushing past him. If he's got an ounce of good sense, he'll follow me.

And he does.

As soon as we're inside our room, I close the door and turn to him.

Panic isn't just written on his face—it's carved.

He's been caught. It's over. Our whole life together . . . done.

"When were you going to tell me?" I ask, fighting back tears.

"When I thought you'd be ready to hear the truth," he says.

"Are you *kidding* me? Who are *you* to decide when *I'm* ready?"

"Because I know you, Nic," he says. "And I know what you've been through."

"For the love of God, I'm not a fucking Fabergé egg." I lift my hands to my temples, squeezing my eyes shut for a moment. "How long?"

He begins to answer, but I cut him off.

"And why were you sending her money from *my* trust?" I ask.

"Because I depleted what savings I had left," he says, collapsing on the edge of the bed and holding his head in his hands. He seems more exhausted than guilty. Maybe carrying a secret this heavy takes a toll on a man's shoulders after a while, but at this point, I couldn't care less.

As soon as I get my answers and we're done here, I never want to see this man again, never want to so much as breathe his name or find him lingering anywhere in my thoughts.

"I don't understand why you've no remorse," I say, releasing an incredulous laugh. "What you've done here is . . . it's beyond, Brant. It's beyond anything I ever would've expected from you."

He glances up at me, his lips moving before he says anything. "How much do you know? Exactly?"

"I know about the money, the phone calls, the woman . . . the daughter," I say.

His left hand drags down the side of his face, and the glint of his meaningless wedding band catches my eye.

"How old is she?" I ask.

He turns to me. "Nine."

An unexpected burn hits my eyes.

"Nine?" I whisper, taking a step back. *"Nine?"*

My breath quickens, and my body grows heavy. My eyes sting with the threat of tears, but I'm too numb with shock to actually cry. How could I have not known?

"Why did you stay with me all this time?" I ask.

He looks to me, brows lifted as if I've insulted him with an idiotic question. "Why wouldn't I? You're my wife. I love you."

I scoff and then glance away. "Yeah. Looks like you really took those vows to heart, didn't you?"

Brant rises, forehead lined as he walks toward me. "Nicolette, what are you talking about?"

His confusion only magnifies my own, but before I have a chance to respond, there's a knock at our bedroom door.

"Nicolette?" It's Wren.

Composing myself, I exchange looks with my husband, and then I get the door. "Hi, sweetheart. What is it?"

"Deputy May is downstairs. She said she needs to talk to us—all of us."

CHAPTER 39

WREN

"Would you like some coffee, Deputy?" Nicolette paces the living room, her fingers dancing together like she's knitting a sweater, and she pulls in lungful after lungful of air but I never hear her release them.

Deputy May lifts her hand before returning it to the belt around her hips. "No thanks."

Sage and I take a seat in the center of the sofa. May says the social worker from the hospital last week is on her way. I haven't seen her since then, and I can't remember her name—only that she smelled heavily of lilacs and talcum powder.

"She's here," Brant says, heading to the entryway to get the door. A second later, the woman with the poufy brown hair and tired-looking eyes is standing next to Deputy May. Nicolette takes a seat beside Sage; Brant takes a seat beside me.

"Girls, you remember Sharon Gable," the deputy says.

I nod and breathe in the heavy scent that invades the room.

Sage's knee bounces, and I place my hand over her thigh to stop it.

"A few days ago," Sharon begins, her words slow, "authorities came across the body of a woman in the woods. They were able to compare her DNA to DNA found at your cabin." She pauses, swallowing. "And I'm so sorry to tell you this, girls, but it was a match."

I glance to Nicolette. "What does this mean?"

Deputy May steps forward. "Your mother is no longer with us."

Sage looks to me, and I slip my arm around her shoulders, letting her bury her head into my shoulder, muffling her sobs. Deep down, beneath all her simplicity, I think she knew just as well as I did that things would never be the way they once were.

Mama never would've abandoned us intentionally, even with all her faults and imperfections.

It's the strangest thing, but . . . I feel nothing.

No sadness. No relief. No sorrow or regret.

Is it normal to feel this numb?

Maybe I'm too angry to feel sad?

"I'm sure you're in shock, girls," May says, "but if you need, we can refer you to a grief counselor . . . someone to talk to."

"What about Evie?" I ask.

The deputy hesitates. "We're still looking for her."

"But, girls," Sharon says, placing her hand on May's shoulder, "there's more."

May won't look at us now.

"What?" I ask. "What else is there?"

"Remember the DNA tests you did at the hospital?" she asks. "When a nurse swabbed the inside of your cheeks?"

"Yes," I say, voice sinking. Heart sinking. Hope sinking. May's normally hardened expression is blank and unreadable. Whatever news she's about to share won't be good.

"The lab wasn't able to get a match between you and your mother," she says, face wincing. "And not only that, but they weren't able to find a match between the two of you."

"What does that mean?" I ask. It wasn't until that day at the hospital that I'd ever heard of such a thing as DNA. "We're not sisters?"

Tears prick the corners of my eyes, but I refuse to let them fall in front of Sage.

"Wren." Sage lifts her head, the tip of her pointed nose flushed and her gaze glassy.

Sharon nods. "I'm so sorry, but yes. That's exactly what that means. Genetically you are unrelated."

"How could that have happened?" Brant asks.

"That's what we're still checking into," Deputy May says. "Normally we'd start by combing through adoption records, but without last names or confirmed birth dates, it's virtually impossible to track those down."

Nicolette covers her nose and mouth with one hand. She's yet to say a single word.

"So what's the next step?" Brant asks.

May looks at us as she answers him. "Next step would be to run their DNA results through the database of the National Center for Missing & Exploited Children and see if we can't get a hit. Right now they're in the process of running DNA tests on some hair strands they found in the cabin that they think belong to the youngest girl. We've also been in contact with the families of missing children in the area, trying to see if we can make any connections."

Nicolette turns to us, reaching across our laps and patting our hands. "I'm so sorry, girls. I know this must be devastating for you."

"Sage," I say, nudging her until she lifts her gaze to mine. "I don't care what some stupid test says. We're still sisters."

Sage offers the tiniest hint of a smile before burying her head into my shoulder all over again. I hold her tighter, as if the harder I squeeze, the more she'll know I'm not going anywhere, and I'll never let her go.

"Do you think . . ." I begin to ask before the words get stuck. "Do you think Mama *kidnapped* us?"

The word is strange and unfamiliar on my tongue, and I didn't know the meaning of it until I started reading that book earlier today.

May shrugs, hesitating. "I don't know the answer to that, Wren. At least not yet."

"There's a chance you were legally adopted," Sharon says, studying us as if she expects a big reaction. "But there's also a chance you weren't . . . and in that case, you might have family looking for you—family that've been looking for you for a very long time."

"Two . . . separate . . . families." My words are whisper soft, but heavy nonetheless.

"One thing at a time, though," Brant says.

"Exactly," Sharon says, sandwiching the palms of her hands together in a silent, gentle clap. "So . . . for now, girls, I just need to know when you want to pay your last respects to your mother."

If it were up to me, it'd be never.

Mama was a liar. And more than likely a thief of the worst kind.

How could Mama, a woman who once cried for days when a mountain lion ran off with one of our newborn goats, steal someone else's child?

I was willing to give her the benefit of the doubt, but that isn't possible now. She isn't here to explain what she did or why she did it. All that's left is a mess of unanswered questions.

I always did find it a little odd the way Mama left to meet The Man one night and came home with a wagon full of supplies and a crying baby wrapped in a blanket made of some bright pink plush material I'd never seen before. At the time, I wasn't quite ten, and I knew nothing about how human babies were born. I was just excited to have a real, live doll to dress and change and feed, and when Mama said she was our new baby sister and she was staying with us forever, I had no reason to question her.

Years later, I tried looking up "pregnancy and childbirth" in one of Mama's medical books, but the section was gone—like it had been ripped clean out. It took a solid year for me to get the courage to ask Mama where babies come from. She was shucking corn by the garden shed, her hands covered in yellow silks and her brow slicked in sweat. She glanced up at me and smiled before saying, "They're a gift, Wren—a gift from God. And gifts come in all sorts of packages. That's the only thing you need to know."

Sage lifts her head from my shoulder. "Can we see her?"

"I'm sorry. No. You won't be able to see her," May says. "Unfortunately, she'd been exposed to the elements for quite a while."

"For how long?" I ask.

"At least a couple of months, if not longer," she says. "I'd have to pull up the coroner's report."

"What happened to her?" My question attracts glances from everyone in the room, Sage included, but I have to know.

The deputy clears her throat. "Blunt force trauma to the head."

"What . . . what does that mean?" I ask, looking to Brant, then to Nicolette, then to Deputy May.

Brant begins to speak, but Deputy May cuts him off. "That's what we say when someone hits another person in the head with an object."

Sage winces. I try to keep a picture from forming in my mind.

"So someone killed her shortly after she left us." My words are mumbled as I try to piece this together. "Someone killed Mama and took Evie." I rise, needing air, needing space. "Evie was sick when they left. *So* sick. Oh, God."

I plaster my hand over my forehead and squeeze my eyes, trying not to picture the worst. Evie needed medical attention, and if Mama never got her to a doctor . . . who knows what became of her?

"Like I said," May tells me, "we won't stop looking until we find her."

CHAPTER 40

Nicolette

I sit with the girls after Deputy May and Sharon Gable leave. Wren's expression is unreadable, her clear eyes frozen as she stares at the floor. I'd give anything to know what's going through her mind right now, if only so I could help her. Sage hasn't stopped weeping, her sweet face buried in her hands. Brant hasn't said a word, though he left for a moment to retrieve a box of tissues from the other room.

My heart aches for them more than I ever could have anticipated. I barely know them, but their pain is real, palpable, and infectious.

The only mother they've ever known is dead.

Evie is still missing.

Their entire world has been turned upside down.

It'd be impossible to so much as attempt to imagine what's going through their minds, so I sit between them, slip my arms around their little shoulders, and offer unspoken sympathy.

"Sage, you should lie down," Wren says, standing. Reaching for her sister's hand, she leads her upstairs, and I hear her say, "I can hold you the way Mama used to if you want me to."

As soon as they're gone, Brant and I lock eyes from across the room, both of us knowing there's a conversation to finish, one that has been simmering for the past half hour.

"I hate to bring this up now . . ." my husband says, "after what just happened, but I think . . . I think you have it all wrong."

Folding my arms across my chest, I ask, "What? What do I have wrong?"

"Do you . . . do you think I *cheated* on you, Nic?" he asks. Brant winces, like this is painful for him, like he's gearing up to play the victim of an unfortunate misunderstanding.

Bullshit.

"Why else would you be sending money to a woman named Beth and hiding a photo of a girl who looks exactly like you? Do you think I'm an imbecile?"

He must if he's been pulling the wool over my eyes for nine damn years.

His mouth twitches up at one side but only for a second.

"Nic . . ." He walks toward me, his arms out. A second later, his hands rest on the sides of my arms. "You have it *all* wrong."

"Then set me straight."

"The little girl?" he asks before pausing a moment. "She's *ours*."

I jerk away from him. He's lying. This isn't possible. A million things I want to say rush through my mind, mingling together and losing their strength in an undercurrent of my anger. I've never felt so disrespected by anyone in my life. For him to think I could possibly believe any of this is the most audaciously manipulative thing my husband has ever done.

My entire body tightens, and while I want to look at Brant, I can't. The mere thought of it makes my stomach twist into a thousand tiny knots, each one a painful reminder that my life—*our* life—has been a lie.

"And Beth in New York," he says, clearly intent on keeping up this charade, "she's the FBI agent assigned to our case. Has been from the beginning. She knows the whole story."

"You're insane if you think I'm going to believe that." I force myself to meet his pathetic gaze, drawn by the rare flavor of desperation in his voice.

He lifts his palms for a moment before letting them fall at his sides. I should be the speechless one. Not him.

"I had a hysterectomy," I remind him, lest he forgot. "I can't get pregnant."

"You *were* pregnant. Once," he says, voice low and gentle. He comes to me, pulling me close despite my arms being crossed tight against my chest. "You didn't know you were. I didn't either. It was one of those . . . I don't know . . . those medically rare things where you were still getting your period and just thought you'd put on a little bit of weight. Plus, with your height, you really didn't show. Anyway, after the delivery, you started hemorrhaging. The doctors couldn't stop the bleeding . . . that's why you had the hysterectomy."

I drag his musky scent into my lungs, sensing the way he studies me like he's looking for a light to go on, something to click, a sign that I remember, that I believe him. But I hold my cards close, not wanting to seem gullible, not wanting to cling to something so far-fetched all because of the earnest look in my husband's watery eyes.

"I came home after running into town one night. You were lying on the bathroom floor in a pool of your own blood, unconscious. Scariest moment of my life, Nic. I called 911." He stares to the side, chewing the inner corner of his bottom lip as he loses himself in thought for a moment. "When we got you to the hospital, they discovered that you were in labor."

"How can a mother have no recollection of giving birth?" I'm not just asking Brant—I'm asking myself. Closing my eyes, I try to force myself to remember something, anything. But everything is blank. I have zero recollections of any of this.

"You were traumatized. Fading in and out of consciousness," he says. "You could have died. *She* could have died. We blinked, and our whole lives had changed. To say it was all surreal would be an understatement. In a lot of ways, it was like a dream. Still feels that way."

"Did I hold her?" I ask, not that I fully believe him yet, but I feel compelled to ask in case it helps to jog my memory. "After she was born?"

His green eyes dampen. "Yeah, Nic. You held her." His expression flattens, and he clears his throat. "That's when you started hemorrhaging. They couldn't get it to stop. Next thing I knew, the room filled with more nurses, and they were wheeling you down to the OR for an emergency hysterectomy."

"I don't understand why I can't recall *any* of this," I say, though I'm trying. I'm trying like hell, fighting through a mental fog I never knew existed—one I'm still not sure exists. I rest my palm against my lower belly, as if that could possibly help me to remember, as if I might possibly feel something I hadn't felt before.

But . . . nothing.

Brant observes me from his side of the room. "I know why you don't, Nic."

"I think a woman would remember giving birth."

"You don't understand," he says before pausing. "You were in shock. Physically. Emotionally. You were exhausted. You were traumatized."

I take a step back and release a short, incredulous laugh. "I'm sorry . . . this just seems so . . ."

I don't finish my thought. I don't need to. He knows I don't buy this.

"I can show you the medical records. I have a copy of your file in my studio—kept them for . . . this . . . I suppose." His eyes plead with mine as he wears a painful wince on his chiseled face. "And you can ask Cate. Or talk to your parents. They'll tell you everything you need to know."

"Cate knew? My parents knew?" The pitch of my voice rises, and the back of my throat burns. I need to remember the girls are upstairs. They don't need to hear us. I don't want to upset them. They've already been through so much.

"Yes, Nic. They know."

"Why would the four of you keep this from me?" I run a hand through my hair, turning away and struggling to breathe despite the massive weight on my chest.

Brant steps toward me, slow and careful. "When we took the baby home, you sometimes forgot about her. You had no recollection of her birth. I had to set timers on your phone so you'd remember to feed her when I was gone. And then you were hearing voices, voices that told you that you were a horrible mother who didn't deserve her."

I clap my hand over my mouth, trying to imagine the young, terrified woman I once was. She feels like a stranger, and trying to recall these things feels as impossible as trying to experience someone else's memories, but my heart goes out to her just the same.

"You cried. Constantly. And when you weren't crying, you were sleeping." Pinching the bridge of his straight nose, Brant continues, "One day that first week, I came home from running to town for more formula, and you were standing at the end of the driveway with the stroller. I thought maybe you'd taken her for a walk, for some fresh air, which I thought was odd because you were supposed to be recovering from your surgery, but it was an unusually warm day for that time of year. Only when I got closer, there was this dead look in your eyes. And when I looked down, the stroller was empty."

"Oh, God."

The nightmares all these years weren't nightmares after all.

They weren't a barren woman's metaphor.

They were *memories*.

"I ran inside, tearing the house apart looking for Hannah—our baby—but she was gone." His voice fractures, and his eyes turn glassy. I've never seen my husband this choked up. "She was only ten days old."

Brant lets me go, taking a seat on the sofa and resting his elbows on his knees.

Hannah.

My gaze scans my husband. Hannah was always the name I'd secretly held in the back of my mind for a someday child. In the early days of our relationship when we'd halfheartedly talk about having kids one day, I refused to mention I'd already chosen names for them. Hannah for a girl, Jonah for a boy. I distinctly recall not wanting to scare him away, not wanting him to think I was one of *those* women who have their entire lives scripted out, and they're just waiting for a man to come along to play the part of their husband.

It makes sense that if we did have a daughter, I'd insist on calling her Hannah.

That, or it's an awfully strange coincidence.

"You said you'd given her to some woman at the park by the woods," he says. "You didn't know her name. You couldn't even remember what she looked like. You said the voices told you to do it."

I take the cushion beside him.

"I'm going to call Cate and ask her," I say.

"By all means." His answer is quick, and he clasps one hand on his knee while the other soars through the air. "In fact, I wish you would so you could see I'm not making any of this up. And while you're at it, I'll grab your file so you can go over all the doctors' reports, the tests, the evaluations."

I tuck a strand of hair behind my ear and swallow the heavy nodule in my dry throat.

Brant has never been one to call my bluff.

He wants me to fact-check everything he's just told me.

I imagine it's an enormous weight off his shoulders, having carried this burden alone for nearly a decade.

"I'll call my parents after," I add. On the off chance the two of them are in on this together, I want him to know I'm going to check under every stone. My parents would never betray me.

"Of course. And you should. We've all been waiting for the right time to tell you this," he says. "Cate thought you should know right away. Your parents and I made the decision to wait a little longer. As the years passed . . . it was easier just to sweep it under the rug a little longer and a little longer. Hannah was gone. What good would it have done to tell you years after the fact? When there was nothing that could be done? When it would only force you to experience that trauma all over again? We'd lost you once, Nic. We were scared to lose you a second time."

Brant covers my hand with his before giving it a soft squeeze.

"Who else knows about this?" I ask, lifting trembling fingers to my lips as our eyes hold. I never knew it was possible to feel guilt and shame over something I have no recollection of doing.

"Everyone, Nic. Everyone knows. We reported her missing," he says. "Your parents came immediately. Cate took the next flight out. The whole town was turned upside down, everyone looking for her."

I'm going to be sick.

All these years, I haven't just been an outsider—I've been the crazy lady who gave her newborn infant to a stranger and carried on like nothing happened.

No wonder they stare.

No wonder they want nothing to do with me.

No wonder I made that woman at the grocery store uncomfortable just by looking at her child.

I'm a monster.

"How could I have done something like this?" I ask. My chest is on fire, my stomach in knots. I don't want to believe this, but while my mind still refuses to remember, my gut tells me Brant speaks the truth. I see it in his eyes. I feel it in the gravity of his words and the invisible heaviness that lingers in the space between us.

"The doctors diagnosed you with postpartum psychosis," he says, "and that, coupled with the traumatic delivery, the stress to your body, the hormonal imbalance from the birth and the hysterectomy . . . and once you realized what you'd done with Hannah . . . you snapped, Nic.

We had you committed at the advice of Dr. Dewdney, and you went voluntarily. You were an inpatient for six weeks while they adjusted your meds until you finally stopped hearing voices. But when you came home, you had no recollection of anything that happened as it pertained to the baby. The doctor said you had dissociative amnesia. It happens when we've been through traumatic events or when we've gone through something overwhelmingly stressful or emotionally painful. He said your mind blocked it out as a coping mechanism. That had a lot to do with why we weren't in a hurry to remind you of what you'd just been through."

It makes sense, then, that he was overly concerned with my staying in New York for the winter—I bet he's lived in silent fear of me having an episode or a breakdown for the past ten years. It was never about the winter blues, always about what had transpired that unusually warm week in December.

"Why didn't they put me behind bars?" I ask. "It has to be some kind of crime to just give your baby away like that."

"You were sick, Nicolette," he says, taking my hands in his. "And that woman, the one who took the baby? She's the criminal here. Not you. She should have called for help. Instead, she took advantage of your situation and stole our child."

My lips tremble. "How could you stand by me after what I did?"

I stare into the sea-green gaze of a man who's held on to an ocean of secrets so turbulent they could have drowned him. It must have pained him to see me carrying on, no recollection whatsoever, while he lived with knowing every last detail of what went down.

If that isn't love, I don't know what is.

"It wasn't always easy," he says. "I'm not going to sit here and tell you that it was. To share everything with you . . . except that? My God, Nicolette, it killed me. But I was willing to live with the pain so you didn't have to. You'd already been through so much. No sense in both of us suffering.

"I love you more than you could ever know, my darling." He buries his face in my lap, a moving sight, and I place my hand on the back of his head, twisting his sandy hair between my fingers before sliding my palm to the side of his face. "Can you forgive me?"

When he glances up, our eyes lock.

"We have to find her." My words quiet to a whisper. Forgiveness is irrelevant. If what he's saying is the truth, he did nothing wrong. The only thing he's guilty of is protecting me from myself.

"All this time, I had no idea if she was still alive. After the leads cooled and the police stopped looking and the FBI agents went back to their posts, Beth would call with updates when she had any. Over the years those calls were fewer and farther between. But two months ago, someone mailed me this picture." Reaching into his wallet, he produces the photo I'd found in his sock drawer. "The age matched up. She looks just like us, Nic. And she's got your same lips, your chin, even your ears. And those eyes? Those are my eyes."

I study the photo, almost as though I'm looking at it for the first time all over again.

And I see it now.

In fact, I'm not sure how I couldn't see it before.

She's just as much me as she is him.

"First came the picture," he says. "Then requests for money. They were extorting me, threatening to remind you about Hannah and about your role in her disappearance—and *I* wanted to be the one to tell you, Nic. I didn't want you to find out this way. I didn't know if it might . . . set you off again."

"So that's why you were taking money from my trust?"

"They said if I paid them, they'd give us Hannah, but then they kept asking for more, dragging it out. At one point Beth wanted to stop because she thought we were being conned, but I refused. I kept looking at that picture, and I knew, Nic. I knew she was ours. And I knew whoever was behind this had to be from the area, had to be someone who knows us. Someone who knows what happened nine years ago and how we've dealt with it."

"You mean how *I* dealt with it."

He says nothing at first. Reluctant to answer or maybe frozen in thought. Then, "Yeah."

"So whoever it is . . . it has to be someone we know?" I ask.

Brant lifts a shoulder. "It could be anyone around here. Everyone in Stillwater knows us, knows what happened, knows that you . . . *forgot*," he says. "I thought I could handle this all on my own and I'd deal with everything else once we had her in our arms again. Everything else seemed so trivial at the time. All I could think about was getting her back."

The photo of the little girl rests between my fingers. I flip it around, studying her angelic face and those haunting, sea-green irises.

"Nic, those pictures that Wren drew," he says, "there was one that looked just like her. Wren said it was her sister. I think there's a chance Evie might be our Hannah." Brant rises, dragging his palm along his smooth jaw as he moves toward one of the windows that overlooks the forest. "Maybe that lady who took her was the same one raising these girls off the grid?"

A raw emptiness burns and swells inside me. I never knew I could miss something this hard, could suffer a void so real and deep.

All this time, I had a daughter.

And I gave her away.

CHAPTER 41

Wren

It's late in the afternoon when we arrive at a funeral parlor that smells like old flowers. Slow, soft music fills my ears, though I have no idea where it's coming from.

"Hello." A silver-haired woman in pearls and a navy pantsuit greets us. "You must be here for Maggie Sharp."

"We are," Nicolette says, speaking for us.

It still doesn't feel right to hear Mama's name. To me, Maggie Sharp is a stranger. And maybe in some ways, so is Mama.

"Right this way." The woman leads us through a couple of doorways toward a simple brown casket covered in white roses. "The community was so touched by your story that they pooled together enough money for you to have this private visitation with your mother. Resting Lawns Cemetery has donated a plot. McCarthy Monument has offered to contribute the headstone of your choosing—whenever you're ready. A person need not have a funeral to be laid to rest."

"Thank you," Nicolette says, speaking for us again.

"I'll be in the office if you need me," she says, voice soft like clouds.

Sage steps toward the casket. "I want to see her."

"I don't think that's a good idea, sweetheart," Nicolette says. "She won't look the way you remember her."

Neither of us has seen a dead body before.

I don't know that I ever want to.

Sage throws her arms over the top of the casket before burying her face into the bend of her elbow. I grab her a tissue from a nearby box.

Part of me wishes I could cry.

This woman fed me, clothed me, loved me, kept me safe my entire life.

Taught me everything I know.

Made me everything that I am.

I should be devastated in this moment . . . not staring at a polished brown box covered in white roses, wondering how much longer we'll be here.

Maybe it'll come later, when my skin stops burning every time I think of a question I'll never be able to ask her, when my fists stop clenching when I think about her promise to protect us, to never let anything happen to us . . . and yet Evie is missing.

I grabbed a slip of paper from a rack in the front of the parlor on our way in. According to this, there are different stages of grief—seven total. And as I read through them, I couldn't help but wonder if it was possible to experience all of them at once.

Or none of them at all.

My heart aches for one more day together: the four of us. The way it was before. Picking lilacs. Singing songs. Feeding the livestock. Playing Old Maid by the fire at night before bed. Mama braiding our hair. Evie's giggles.

But it'll never happen.

And it's all Mama's fault.

"I'll be waiting in the car," Nicolette says. "Take as much time as you need."

◆ ◆ ◆

Sage sleeps the whole drive home with her head on my shoulder, and I stare out the window, thinking about Evie. Where she is. Who she's with. If she's smiling, or if she's scared. If she's missing us . . .

After a while, it hurts too much to think about, so my mind wanders to the blonde woman. If Mama wasn't my biological mother, maybe she was? I wish I knew if she was looking for me, if she missed me. I try to imagine a mother and a father and a warm house, cousins and aunts and uncles, the kinds of things that everyone else around here seems to have.

And then I try to imagine Sage's family, my chest tightening when I think about how weird it is that we come from two different families. Two sets of parents. Two sets of aunts and uncles and cousins. Are they looking for her, too?

By the time we pull into the Gideons' garage, Sage stirs awake, glancing around like she just emerged from a heavy dream and has no idea where she is.

"Are you girls hungry?" Nic asks as we climb out and head inside.

"No, thank you," I say, inhaling the distinct scent of the Gideon home. I don't think I could describe it any other way than pleasant. Every once in a while, I can catch a single note—sometimes lemon, sometimes cinnamon; other times the scent of her laundry room fills the halls, and I stop for a moment, wondering if I'll remember the way this house smelled long after I've gone from here.

I don't expect the Gideons to let us stay here forever.

Sage says nothing, tromping upstairs to our room in a sleepy haze.

Lingering in the hallway, I decide some time spent sketching in Brant's office might take the edge off today, so I head upstairs, swiping my sketch pad and pencil from the dresser in the guest room.

A moment later, I'm showing myself into Brant's office and adjusting the drafting stool by the window to the perfect height when something catches my eye.

A photograph rests on Brant's end of the desk, only it isn't just any photograph.

It's a photograph of Evie.

How would they have this? Why would they have this? It's recent, of that I'm certain. She looks exactly the same as the last time I saw her.

My lungs expand, my chest rises and falls, but still, I struggle to breathe. It only takes a moment for me to catch my breath, to calm myself enough to set my thoughts straight. If they have this picture, they might know where she is. They might know something I don't. This could be a good thing.

I don't want to think about the alternative.

With her picture carefully clutched against my chest, I run downstairs to demand an explanation.

CHAPTER 42

NICOLETTE

"The person extorting us expects another transfer tomorrow, but Western Union doesn't open until nine," Brant tells me as we wash up for bed that night. It's a couple of hours earlier than we normally wind down, but given the news we just broke to Wren about Evie possibly being our missing daughter, we're too exhausted to do anything else. "And you've frozen the account."

I press a hot towel against my face, and when I meet my own gaze in the mirror, all I keep picturing is the look on Wren's face when she dashed down the stairs earlier with Hannah's picture in her hand.

She took the news with skepticism, like the intelligent girl she is, first implying that we knew where her sister was, that we were hiding information from her, but Brant set her straight. He answered every question she asked with poise and tact, not once letting his true emotions break through.

By the end of our discussion, her demeanor had softened when it hit her that we were her best chance at finding Evie. And that Evie was very much presumed to be alive.

"What happens if we don't pay?" I ask out of curiosity, not that I'd be willing to find out.

Our gazes intersect in the mirror.

"I don't know. I've yet to take that chance."

Earlier today, after I'd finished a two-hour phone call with my parents so they could corroborate Brant's story, he pulled me into his office, and we pored over medical records and documents that he fished out of a cabinet in the corner—including Hannah's birth certificate and all the letters and threats this extortionist has been sending for the past couple of months.

Whoever it is . . . they know *everything*.

No wonder Brant took this so seriously.

"What exactly is the FBI doing to find her? Beth is in the city, right?"

"One of their agents is some expert survivalist tracker-locator type. I guess he's been on assignment here since we got the first letter and it was obvious it was someone who knew us. Beth said he went around talking to people here, watching, looking for suspicious activity. Something tipped him off, and then he insisted on searching the woods. As far as we know, he's been in the forest for weeks now, but Beth hasn't heard from him in a while. He's supposed to check in on his satellite phone every so often, but I'm not sure when he last called."

"She's not concerned?" I ask, sliding into bed and situating the covers, though I'm not sure how I'm going to get any sleep tonight.

"Doesn't seem like it. She said he knows what he's doing and he's one of the best." He climbs in next to me.

Leaning back against my cool pillow, I stare at the ceiling, at the motionless fan above. "So what now?"

Brant slides his hand under the sheets, finding mine. "We don't stop until we have her in our arms again."

CHAPTER 43

Wren

It's been three days since we said our goodbyes to Mama.

Sage cried until her tears dried up, and then she cried some more, soft whimpers in her sleep mostly. But this morning was a different story.

Nicolette got the call around eight.

There was a hit on Sage's DNA. A match, they said.

They'd found Sage's family, and they'd been looking for her all this time.

They also regretfully informed us that there were zero hits on my DNA.

"How do I look, Wren?" my sister asks, combing her bangs down her forehead.

"Lovely," I tell her.

"What do you think they're like?"

"I bet they're nice. And I bet you look just like them."

She smiles. With her dark hair and fine features, she always stuck out like a sore thumb alongside Mama, Evie, and me.

"Girls?" Nicolette stands in the doorway of our room. "They're going to be here any minute. Just wanted to check on you."

Sage bites her lip, looking to me. "I want to meet them, Wren, but I don't want to leave you."

Blinking away tears, I force a smile. "Everything's going to be okay no matter what happens."

I don't know if that's true, but I do know those are the only words she needs to hear right now.

Heading downstairs, we take a seat on the sofa. I grab my latest book off the coffee table, and Sage holds the baby doll I made her the other week, staring ahead in complete silence.

"Wren?" she asks.

"Yeah?"

"What's going to happen to you after this?"

Glancing to the side so she doesn't see the well of tears rimming my eyes, I say, "I don't know."

"Nic, they're here," Brant calls from the kitchen.

Nicolette strides toward the entryway, and my sister reaches for my hand. Her palm is hot and damp.

A moment later the sound of footsteps and voices carries toward us, and when Brant and Nicolette step aside, a man and woman, both on the smaller side and slender, much like Sage, stand frozen by the front door.

"Mark." The woman cups her hands over the lower half of her face, eyes squinting over her hands like she's about to cry. "It's her. It's Emma."

His lower lip quivers, and he places his hands on her shoulders, giving them a squeeze.

"Please. Come in," Brant reminds them since they haven't taken another step. "Make yourselves at home."

Sage's mother falls to her knees in front of us, her hands clinging to Sage's hips, then lifting to her shoulders, then her hair, as if she needs to feel that she's real and not a mirage. Her dad is more reserved, standing back and trying his hardest to be strong even though his eyes tell a different story.

"You were just a baby," her mother says, eyes searching her daughter's. "We were at the park here in town—in Stillwater Hills. I'd set you down on a yellow blanket and given you your three o'clock bottle, and then I went to push your brothers on the swings. I was only gone a minute . . . when I came back . . . you were gone." Fat tears slide down her pale cheeks, and she dabs at them with the back of her hand. "Just like that. Nothing left but that yellow blanket."

Sage offers an apologetic smile, even though none of this is her fault. I wonder if she feels a connection to her mother? If she can feel the pain of being missed?

"We looked for you for years," the mom continues. "And finally, it got to be too much. Your father took a job in Vermont. We needed to get away from Stillwater Hills, start fresh. Even the police told us to stop looking after several years, that we were wasting our time."

She reaches for Sage's face again, her fingertips grazing Sage's skin like she's a delicate china doll.

"You have two brothers back home," she says with a gentle smile. "They can't wait to meet you. And you have grandparents and aunts and uncles and cousins."

Despite the weight sinking into my chest and the burn in my eyes, I'm happy for her.

I am.

"We'll be staying in town with your grandparents for the next few weeks," the mother tells her. "Dr. Pettigrew thought it'd be best if we transitioned you back into the family gradually, maybe with some counseling and some family therapy?" She looks to me. "I know how close you are to your sister, and we don't want you to think we're taking you away from her and never looking back." She turns back to Sage. "I promise you, Emma—Sage—your sister will always be your sister. We'll do everything we can to make sure you can see her anytime you want."

"Thank you." Sage's voice is a breathy squeak.

"Would you like to meet the rest of your family?" her father asks, his hands squeezing his wife's shoulders as if the anticipation of her answer is more than he can bear.

Sage's eyes fill with tears once more—but these tears are happy ones. I think. And she says nothing, but I know what she's wanting.

"Go," I say, fighting watering eyes with a smile. "Be with them."

"You were right, Wren. You were right this whole time," she says, throwing her arms around me. "Everything's going to be okay."

CHAPTER 44

NICOLETTE

Brant slides his phone into his pocket. "That was Beth. Remember that survivalist guy she hired?"

"Yes."

"He's on his way over. Guess he just touched base with her an hour ago and he's in the area, so he wants to stop by and go over his findings face-to-face."

I clean up what's left of our supper dishes and wipe down the counters. Wren's in the next room, nose buried in her tenth book this week, and Sage is in town spending time with her family. It's been five days since they reunited. They've been picking her up around eight every morning and bringing her home just past dinnertime, though as she grows more comfortable with them, she might start staying overnight at her grandparents'. For now, our house is still her landing pad, a safe, familiar place for her to recuperate from all that has happened. As exciting and chaotic as this time is for her, Dr. Pettigrew says having Wren to come home to is paramount to her successful transition.

"When's he going to be here?" I ask.

Brant glances out the window by the table. "Now."

Smoothing my hands down my sides, I clear my throat and head to the door. Brant follows.

"You must be Chuck," my husband says when he answers.

The man standing on the other side is large, bearish almost, his face razor nicked and his hair shower damp. The scent of hotel soap wafts off him, barely covering his musky scent.

"Come on in." I move out of the way, and the man begins to unbutton his coat as he passes the threshold. "Would you like something to drink?"

"No, thank you, ma'am," he says, lifting a palm. A moment later he glances toward the family room, eyes landing on Wren. "Jesus."

Before I have a chance to process what's going on, our quiet Wren begins to scream, her legs scrambling as she climbs up the back of the sofa, trying to get as far away from him as possible.

"Don't let him take me." Wren drops her book, and I run to her side, taking her hand.

"What's wrong?" I ask, wrapping my arms around her and pulling her down to a seat cushion.

"That's him . . . the man who broke into our cabin and said he was going to take us."

"Here. Come with me," I say, guiding her to the next room. When I rub my palm against her back, I swear I can almost feel the erratic thumping of her little heart. "He's an FBI contractor. A tracker. He was hired to find Evie. Wren, did he hurt you? Did he touch you in some way?"

She exhales, brows meeting. "No. He just said he was going to take us. And he kept asking about Mama."

"I can imagine how traumatic that experience was for you and I don't agree with his tactics, but I promise you, Wren, I won't let him near you."

Her eyes study mine, perhaps searching for the truth, and a moment later she nods.

"Why don't you go upstairs for a bit?" I propose. "I'll call for you when he's gone."

I watch her leave before heading back to the other room.

I take a seat across from Chuck, crossing my legs. "So? What do you have for us?"

His brawny physique fills the entirety of our leather club chair, and he pitches himself forward, like he's unable to get comfortable.

Clearing his throat, he says, "I'm sure Beth told you I located the cabin."

Brant nods. "Yes, this morning."

"I was able to determine it was, in fact, the cabin of the woman I was looking for—but I couldn't determine if your daughter was a part of that circus because the woman and the youngest girl were gone. The two older girls who were there thought I was going to kill them, so they wouldn't tell me a damn thing." His tone turns salty, and he pauses. "A few days in, they drugged me and snuck out of the cabin with my bag. Took me a bit longer to get back to town, thanks to some bad meat I was forced to eat since they stole my MREs. Sidelined me for a few days out there, and on top of that, it was a little hard without, you know . . . my bailout bag. Tarpaulins, compass, water purification tabs, canteen, flint . . . they grabbed it all, then ran. Left me for dead."

He almost laughs, like he's impressed, and then he stops himself.

"You terrified them," I say. "Can you blame them for running away?"

"I have that effect on people. Anyway, I never would've hurt them. Was actually planning on taking them to town with me. They were going to die out there all alone, barely any food, winter setting in. So back to this, the only thing of interest I was able to find in the cabin were a couple of death certificates. Ray Sharp and Imogen Sharp. Both passed away about twenty years ago."

"I'm sorry." I stop him. "How did you know to look for Maggie Sharp in the first place?"

"Beth assigned me here to scope the place out after Brant got that first letter. Spent some time in your little town, talked to a lot of locals, asked about any recluses or any people to watch out for," he says. "One person mentioned the name Maggie Sharp. Said she was a local second-grade teacher who lost her husband and daughter in some hit-and-run accident when they were walking home from the park. Guess she went crazy after that. Was never the same. Said she was a recluse, and then after a while, no one ever saw her again."

"Maggie Sharp." Brant says her name softly. "Never heard of her."

Maggie Sharp.

The mental picture I had of the kind of woman she was distorts and softens, and I find it harder to picture a crazed, ill-intentioned woman and easier to picture a distraught, heartbroken mother who couldn't save her child . . . but maybe she saw me and saw her second chance to save a child from what she perceived as harm?

I imagine two mothers, both traumatized, both thinking they were doing the right thing at the time, and my heart aches—for both of us.

"Anyway, a few weeks ago, I was at some little shop on your square, and I spot this guy buying a few random items—toothpaste, a comb, you know. The cashier asked if he wanted his usual order, said it was ready to go, and pointed to a stack with some floral-print fabric, crayons, stuff that clearly wasn't for him. He told her he wouldn't be needing those anymore and got the hell out of there. After that, I followed him home, set up some surveillance, monitored all the comings and goings. But it was only ever him. Guy was unquestionably a bachelor." Chuck's eyes light, and he leans forward. "Anyway, it wasn't long after that, I watched him carrying a box of these little soaps tied in purple twine inside the supermarket. Guess he sold them there or something. Took a closer look at it and saw how pretty it was. There was no way that guy was making and selling artisanal goat-milk soaps, so right then and there I knew he was working with someone and—"

"Hold on." Brant cocks his head at me. "Davis."

The soaps. Lavender-scented. Goat's milk. Tied in lilac-colored string.

His brother claimed to be selling them for a friend of his, and Brant would always buy a bar here or there out of sheer kindness and to support what he believed were local artisans.

I gasp. "Your brother."

"That son of a bitch." Brant stands, the indentation beneath his cheekbone pulsing. When his eyes snap on to mine, he tries to speak, but nothing comes out.

He's in shock.

I'm not surprised.

Davis was always jealous of our financial situation. Always asking for loans and handouts. Always making snide comments. Always making Brant feel as though his success was undeserved, dumb luck. It wouldn't be far-fetched to imagine Davis exploiting an opportunity to inflict pain on his brother.

"Yes. Your brother." Chuck sniffs as he laughs, rubbing his scarred chin. "Anyway, your words, not mine."

"I don't understand. How did you know to go into the forest?" I ask.

"I'm getting there," Chuck says, pointing a meaty finger. "All the times I'd searched his property, it was when he was at work, so it was always in the dark. One morning, he came home stumbling drunk around nine in the morning, probably stopped off at the bar on his way home. Gave him twenty minutes to pass out and decided to take my chances. And good thing I did. Found a little clearing just behind his trailer. Plain as day, I saw a worn path, almost like something with wheels was using it because the ruts were small but deep in parts. Sure as hell wasn't shoes that did that. So then I got to thinking about the soaps he was selling . . . followed the path, saw it went deeper and deeper . . ."

I've heard enough—for now. "How do we get Hannah?"

"So what are you saying? That Davis has some part in this?" Brant asks Chuck. "Why wouldn't Beth have said something?"

"You'll have to talk to her about that," Chuck says. "But more than likely, I imagine she was working to make sure the two of you weren't in cahoots in any way, didn't want you tipping him off."

My husband begins to protest. I know him, and Chuck's comment has offended him to his core, but I place my hand on his arm in hopes to keep him from saying something he'll regret.

"We have to go," Brant says as he stands and pats his pockets for his keys. "Now."

"No." I grab his arm. "We have to call Deputy May."

Davis has guns. And zero qualms about using them. His entire acreage on the outskirts of town is littered with "No Trespassing" signs.

"Your brother is insane," I remind him. "You're not going there without the police."

Rushing to the kitchen, I grab the slip of paper with Deputy May's personal cell number and yank my phone off the charger. Before I have a chance to dial her number, Chuck appears behind me.

"If you're calling the police, I'm pretty sure they're already there," he says. "Beth was on her way last I talked to her."

Everything's happening so fast, and yet it's not happening fast enough.

CHAPTER 45

WREN

There's an unusual amount of commotion coming from downstairs, so much so that I can't focus on the sketch I'm drafting—a picture of the three of us sisters. I want to give it to Sage before she goes to her new home in Vermont in a few weeks.

Placing my pencil down, I make my way to the top of the stairs.

Deputy May is here.

And the stranger from the cabin is still here. He hasn't left.

Nicolette and Brant are talking so fast I can hardly understand them, and they keep pacing back and forth, passing the stair landing time and again. Going from the kitchen to the living room and back.

With a clammy hand clenching the banister, I make my way downstairs.

"Wren." Nicolette stops pacing the foyer when she sees me.

"What's going on?" I take a look around and thank my lucky stars that that brute is seated a good distance away from me. Nicolette's eyes are bloodshot, and her hair is a mess, like she's been running her fingers through it, pulling and tugging at the ends. This isn't her. This isn't the Nicolette I've come to know. Dragging in a sharp breath, I ask, "Did you find Evie? You did, didn't you?"

Brant and Nicolette exchange looks.

"No," Brant says. "Not yet."

"Then what is this?" I ask. "Why is Deputy May here?"

"We have a lead," Deputy May says. "We're just going to go check it out, Wren. We'll let you know if anything comes of it."

"I'm coming with you." I begin to make my way to the back door, where my shoes rest on the rug, but I'm stopped by the collective "no" coming from the group.

"You're going to be safer here," Nicolette says. "I'll give you the code to the security system. It's too dangerous for you out there."

I could scream.

For the first time, Nicolette sounds like Mama.

"No." My voice is so loud it startles everyone into silence. "She's my sister. I'm coming with you."

"Wren, it's not a good idea. I'm sorry, but you—" the deputy begins to say, only I won't hear it.

"I'm going with you," I say, each word spoken through gritted teeth. "You're not leaving me behind. I don't care how unsafe you think it is. I'm not a child."

Brant and Nicolette share a glance with each other.

"I know you're not a child, sweetheart, but we just want to keep you safe," Nicolette says, trying to soothe me with her voice.

"If Evie's there, I need to be there." I've never talked back to Nicolette or disrespected her wishes in her home, but I refuse to be kept from my sister. "She's going to want to see a familiar face, don't you think?"

Brant stands aside as he watches his wife, and all of them are quiet for a moment.

"Fine," Deputy May says. "But you're staying in my squad car the entire time. You're not to set one foot outside of it until I say it's safe to do so, do you understand?"

I'll settle for that. "Yes."

The next moment becomes a blur of keys and engines and doors and locks, and by the time it's over, we're loaded up: me with May, and Brant driving Nicolette and the man whom I've learned is named Chuck.

The early evening moon paints the sky in beautiful shades of deep blue with puffy white clouds still visible in the dark, but all I can focus on is the steady hum the car makes against the gray road.

Ten minutes later, we're parked in front of a blue house that's long and skinny, with white metal around the bottom. There's no garage, no vehicle of any kind sitting outside. Just a shed and a small wooden porch by the door on the side.

May radios for backup before climbing out of the car.

"Remember, stay here," she tells me before shutting the door.

With her hand on her belt, she approaches the rotting wooden porch, climbs the steps, and then raps on the door.

I glance at Brant and Nicolette in their car, Nicolette biting her painted nails and Brant's jaw flexing as he watches. No one blinks. No one moves.

A moment later, May steps away, heading to the Gideons' car. I can't make out what's being said, but I don't need to. Her furrowed brow and downturned lips say it all.

The house is dark.

No one's home.

My sister isn't here.

CHAPTER 46

Nicolette

"We pinged him off a cell tower about five miles from here," May says, leaning into Brant's car window as we wait, parked outside Davis's trailer.

I glance toward her squad car, making eye contact with Wren. "I should check on her."

Climbing out of the passenger side, I'm met with the sound of a second door. Fully expecting Brant to try to stop me, to tell me to get back inside where I'm safer, I'm shocked to find it isn't Brant at all.

It's Chuck, and he's headed toward the house.

"What are you doing?" I ask, stopping to watch as he strides with the confidence of a man who's never known fear a day in his life. A moment later, he disappears around the back of the trailer. Perimeter check, perhaps? When he emerges, he heads straight for the trash, flinging the lid open and reaching inside.

"Hey, May, get a look at this," Chuck says, holding up a colorful box. "Kid's meal. Isn't that old either—there's mail in this trash bag from two days ago. Think I just found your probable cause."

My heart bounds in my chest as I look to Brant. May brings her radio to her lips.

"We've got unmarked cars at every road leading up here, and we've blocked every exit. If he tries anything, he won't get very far," she says, heading back to the house. "Anyway, I'm going to need you to get back into your car."

Running back to our idling sedan and climbing in, I watch from behind Brant's dash as May kicks in the front door and disappears inside, swallowed by the dark.

Reaching for Brant's hand, I nearly claw my nails into his flesh while we wait, at times forgetting to breathe.

A minute passes.

Then another.

And another.

My hope withers, but it doesn't fade completely.

Glancing down the highway outside Davis's property, I focus on the distance, half-expecting him to roll up and do something crazy when he sees us here.

"Nic." Brant's elbow jerks against my arm. A second later he's climbing out of the driver's side, his gaze transfixed on something. I follow his stare.

Standing on the rickety side porch is Deputy May, holding the hand of a little blonde girl rubbing the sleep out of her eyes.

Flinging the door open, I chase after Brant.

Wren follows.

Everything happens in slow motion, and I can't take my eyes off that sweet face of hers, a face that feels strangely familiar and makes me cast away any and all doubts I held until this moment.

"That's our daughter," I whisper into cupped hands once I come to a stop next to my husband.

"That's our daughter." His voice is broken; he doesn't blink.

Hand in hand, we go to her, to Evie—our Hannah—racing across Davis's gravel driveway toward the leaning porch, where the sweet angel shields her eyes from our pointed headlights. As soon as we get within a few yards of her, Deputy May shakes her head and places her palm toward us, stopping us from coming any closer, and it's then that I remember that this isn't a joyous reunion . . . not for the little girl at the center of it all.

She's ours, but we're not hers, not yet. As of now, we're strangers. The only mother she's ever known is gone forever. And who knows what Davis has put her through these last several months.

"Evie!" Wren's voice comes from behind us, and the moment their eyes meet, Evie releases May's hand and runs to her sister.

Sirens sound in the distance, and May reaches for her radio, bringing it closer to her ear.

Before we get the chance to fully appreciate the joyful expression on our daughter's face and this long-overdue reunion, the sear of bright headlights almost blinds us, and flashes of red and blue paint the front of Davis's trailer.

Tires skid to a stop in his gravel driveway, walling the scene in a cloud of rock dust, and Evie hides behind Wren, tucking herself out of sight, and Brant shields me.

Everything happens at once.

The door to Davis's truck swings open, and a moment later, when the dust settles, I'm able to distinguish the outline of his hands in the air against the flicker of the squad car's light bar behind him. Two officers guard themselves behind open car doors, guns pointed, and three more swarm Davis's truck.

May yells for us to get down.

Before I so much as blink, Davis is on the ground, his face planted in grit and gravel while one of the deputies cuffs his wrists behind his back.

"Nic, come on." Brant leads me to our car, walking me to the passenger side, all the while keeping his vision trained on the situation by the truck.

"You're not going over there, are you?" I ask before climbing in, but he doesn't hear me. "Brant."

"Just get in the car. I'll be back."

I've been married to him long enough to recognize the corded-steel look in his eyes, but before I have an opportunity to protest, he's gone.

Stepping out of the car, I slam the door behind me and trail after my husband, but he's already halfway down the driveway, headed straight to one of the patrol units, where a squat deputy is shoving Davis in the back seat with minimal effort. Davis is gaunter than usual—a sign he's using again—and he doesn't put up a fight, doesn't so much as resist. But he was always more of a manipulative weasel than a fighter.

"Brant," I call after my husband, who won't acknowledge me, and from several yards back, I watch him say something to the deputy, who then nods and leaves the back door to the squad car open.

In an instant, my husband lunges at his brother, fisting his shirt and dragging him out of the car. Davis lands on his knees in a cloud of dust, his hands still secured behind him.

"Look at me, you piece of shit," my husband commands him.

It takes a moment, but eventually Davis lifts his head.

"You knew where she was this entire time?" Brant's voice is low, but I still hear him loud and clear. A couple of deputies keep their backs toward the situation, and another one is by the leaning porch, talking to May, who's suddenly taking an interest in what's going on but doesn't appear anxious to come any closer. They're all turning a blind eye.

Davis spits to the side, defiant in his choice not to answer. Even his current state of physical restraint doesn't stop him from trying to get one more rise out of his brother.

"How long?" Brant's voice is deeper, grittier.

Davis shrugs a shoulder before scratching his nose against it. "I don't know. The years tend to blend together any—"

"How long?" Brant crouches, getting in his face.

Davis laughs. And I'm sure under any other circumstances, this would be a sight to see—my sweet-natured husband roughing up his brother—but the chuckle is all the incentive Brant needs to grab Davis by his shirt and lift him just enough before letting him drop. This time he falls on his back, his knees bent at a ninety-degree angle. Brant's going to destroy Davis. He's going to destroy him in front of everyone.

Brant is all the family Davis has left. Everyone else is long gone, and the ones who aren't severed ties with Davis years ago when he started getting into drugs and running around with the wrong crowd. It wasn't long before Davis started looking like the older of the two. Bags under his cloudy eyes, teeth in desperate need of fixing, skin sallow and washed out. We always knew when he was clean. And when he wasn't.

But all this time and after all the antics Davis pulled, Brant has never once considered turning his back on his brother, choosing to remember the one he knew, the one he grew up with, the one with whom he rode bikes, traded baseball cards, and camped under the stars in the summer when it was hotter inside their house than it was outside. Davis was the one who bought him his first camera from a local pawnshop on his thirteenth birthday, who encouraged him to take pictures and even let him practice on him. Photography became Brant's escape as well as a way to control his chaotic reality. In the end, it became so much more than a hobby or a passion. It was a way of survival.

He's never said it, but I believe Brant feels indebted to Davis for this reason. And I think that's why he's always been so quick to give and even quicker to forgive.

But as I watch my husband's shoulders tighten now, watch the lines between his brows deepen, and see the flex of his teeth grinding as he stands over his brother, I know after this, Davis is dead to him.

"Why?" Brant asks. His green eyes shift as he searches his brother's face. If he's looking for a sign of remorse, he won't find it there.

"I took good care of her," Davis says, as if that changes anything. "She was fed. Got to watch cartoons all day. Hell, she was living the good life."

Brant begins to speak but stops, his clenched fist lifting to the air and his lips pursing. He turns to me, shaking his head.

"He's not worth it," I say. And he never was. We loaned him thousands upon thousands of dollars, bought him vehicles when he had no other way to get to work, and bailed him out of jail more times than I can count on one hand. Not once did we get a thank-you—and now this . . .

"Why?" Brant asks once more, his voice hardened and edgy.

"Do I really have to answer that?" Davis finally says. "Come on, Brant. You're not stupid."

"If it was money you wanted, why didn't you just ask? Hasn't stopped you from asking any other time."

"Shit, haven't I asked you enough? Gets stale. This way was win-win. You get your daughter back; I get to pad my bank account." Davis's attention shifts to me. "And I could tell Nic was starting to get tired of breaking out the old checkbook. You were pulling back, Brant. You were starting to hesitate and make excuses. That well was bound to dry up eventually."

The last time Davis asked for a loan, Brant put his foot down of his own volition. As difficult as it was sometimes, I always bit my tongue when it came to financial matters between them. As far as I knew, the money Davis had been siphoning from Brant came from Brant's personal account—never my trust.

"You disgust me." My husband spits his words. "You're sick, you know that?"

"I never hurt her. Just so you know. Told her I was her uncle. She got three square meals a day and all-she-could-watch cartoons."

"I'm done," Brant says as he gets in Davis's face one more time. *"Done."*

Davis begins to laugh, but it's cut short the second Brant delivers a swift kick into the side of his stomach. Writhing, he rolls to his side, knees curling in, and I spot the shorter deputy turn toward the commotion.

"We done here?" she asks my husband as she shuffles back. Her pointer finger passes between the two of them.

A black SUV arrives, and out from the driver's seat climbs a petite brunette with a shield hanging from her neck. Beth, perhaps? A man steps out from the passenger seat. Deputy May makes her way across the gravel the moment they spot one another.

Brant's chest lifts and sinks, and his hands rest on his hips. A thin sheen of sweat collects across his brow. Sliding my arm into the bend of his elbow, I pull him away from his traitorous flesh and blood and back toward the flesh and blood that's going to need us from this moment on.

"It's over," I say, resting my head against his shoulder as we walk back to May and the girls. *"It's over."*

CHAPTER 47

Wren

"Scoot," I say to Evie as I return to her hospital room.

She smiles, making room for me in her bed. We've been here almost a full day now, doctors and nurses flitting in and out of here asking hundreds of questions and doing dozens of tests.

Evie changes the stations of the TV like she's done it a million times before.

"How'd you get so good at this?" I ask.

"The Supply Man let me watch cartoons. He gave me my own TV. And he got me toys, too."

From what I've heard her tell the doctors and staff here, he didn't hurt a single hair on her head—all he did was keep her in a locked room, only letting her out to use the bathroom when he wasn't at work.

And if that wasn't mind-boggling enough, he even got her medicine.

"Where's Mama, Wren?" Evie asks.

No one's told her yet.

"Do you remember much about that night when you were sick and Mama carried you through the woods?" I ask.

Evie bites her full lower lip and shakes her head. "No. I just remember waking up in the Supply Man's house."

I don't know how to tell her Mama's gone, and she's in such good spirits I'm afraid to break it to her right here, right now.

"Wren, he knew everything about us," Evie says like it's a good thing. It strikes me now that our entire existence was spent living in a prison of sorts. Keeping her in a locked room probably wasn't all that traumatic for her. And the toys and cartoons surely helped. "He said he's known Mama for a long time, and they go way back. Our house, Wren? It was his old hunting cabin. He gave it to Mama so we'd have a place to live. Wasn't that so kind of him?"

I wonder if he knew all along that Mama took us or if she let it slip, thinking he was an old friend whom she could confide in and trust. Obviously she trusted him for a lot of years if he was always bringing our supplies and selling our products for us.

"Where's Sage?" Evie asks.

"You'll see her soon." Leaning back against the pillow beside her, I roll to my side, brushing wisps of her blonde hair from her face. "So much to tell you, Evie."

I slip my arm behind her shoulders.

For now, I just want to smell her, feel her, hold her, and never let her go.

CHAPTER 48

Nicolette

Dr. Pettigrew takes us to an empty conference room at the end of the hospital hallway. Seated at the end of a long table, she opens a manila folder and flips a piece of white paper toward us.

Brant takes my hand. I hold my breath.

"Results are in," she says, rose-colored lips twitching. "She's your daughter."

The two of us collapse against one another, and my husband's arms surround me.

I knew. He knew. But to hear it—to see it—makes it all the more real.

"When should we tell her?" Brant asks.

For the past thirty-six hours, we've kept Evie company in the hospital, ensured she was comfortable, and been involved in every aspect of her care—as much as the hospital would allow. But without legal proof that she's ours, we were forced to keep our distance. When she wondered who we were, Wren told her we were a couple of kindhearted people who took her in and wanted to help them.

Pettigrew lifts her left brow. "Honestly? The sooner the better. And I'm more than happy to facilitate that conversation."

"I'd like to tell her myself," I say, my gaze floating between theirs. "This whole thing happened because of me."

Those words are heavier on the outside than the inside. Saying them out loud instead of thinking about them gives them more weight, makes them real. I haven't had time yet to process any of this, to properly deal with my guilt and the guilt that's going to wash over me in waves the more I get to know my daughter, but all I can do is take it one day at a time and lean on my husband when things get too intense.

"But it wasn't your fault, Nic." Brant reaches across the table, placing his hand over mine. "You were sick. You've got to stop blaming yourself."

"Easier said than done," I tell him.

The warmth of his hand over mine as his peaceful green eyes offer me serenity reminds me that Hannah isn't the only person I've wronged in all this.

I never should have doubted him. I never should have assumed the worst from the person who loves me most in this world.

I'll tell him that, and I'll spend the rest of my life making it up to him, but first things first.

"So do we just . . . lead in with anything in particular, or how should we approach this?" Brant asks.

Dr. Pettigrew's lips bunch together as she concentrates. "Be as direct as you can without making yourself uncomfortable. Speak from the heart. There's not going to be an easy or perfect way to tell her what happened, but as her biological parents and soon-to-be custodial parents, it's important that she understands what happened and why she's going to live with you."

Rising from my chair, I tug my blouse into place.

"Ready?" I ask Brant.

He stands, nodding.

"Would you like me to join you?" the doctor asks.

"I don't think so," I say. "But thank you."

She nods, and I meet Brant around the other side of the table, slipping my hand into his. Together we return to the other end of the hall, knocking lightly before showing ourselves into Evie's room.

Wren is lying next to her on the bed, the two of them laughing at the cartoons flickering across the screen.

"Wren, could you give us a moment with Evie?" Brant asks, clearing his throat.

Wren sits up, brushing her hair back into place, before padding out of the room and closing the door.

Evie sits up, watching the two of us, her smile fading.

Pushing chairs to either side of her bed, we situate ourselves. Brant gives me a nod, and I force the heated flush from my ears, gathering my thoughts.

"Evie, do you know who we are?" I ask.

"You're Brant and Nicolette," she says. "You're the people that are helping Wren."

"Right, but we're more than that," I say. "When you leave here tomorrow, you're going to come home with Wren, to our house . . . which will be your house."

Her blonde brows meet. "I don't understand."

"Your mama," I say, "the one who raised you . . . she isn't who you thought she was."

"What?" she asks.

"She kidnapped you. All three of you," I say gently. "Do you know what that means?"

She shakes her head.

"You didn't belong to her. She stole you from your mothers and raised you as her own." I want so badly to reach out, brush her fine, blonde hair away from her striking green eyes, cup her sweet little hand beneath mine. All in due time, I suppose. "It gets a little more complicated than that, and one of these days we'll sit down and tell you everything you could ever want to know, but basically, Evie . . . she took you from me when you were five days old."

And that's exactly the way the police describe it. They said it was a kidnapping since I wasn't in the right frame of mind and couldn't have willingly given up my baby.

Evie's gaze moves to the cartoon on the TV.

"Where's Mama?" she asks a moment later. I imagine she needs more time to process everything I've just said, therapy with Dr. Pettigrew, immersion in her new normal. It's going to be a long road, but studying my daughter's gorgeous green gaze, I'm filled with nothing short of hope.

Miracles happen every day.

I'm looking at one right now.

"I'm so sorry, sweetheart," I say, my hand aching to take hers. "She got hurt very badly in the woods, and she's no longer . . . with us."

Evie turns to me after a quiet moment, lip quivering. "She's dead?"

"Yes, sweetheart. I'm so sorry."

My daughter begins to cry over the only mother she ever knew, and I can't help myself. I climb into the bed beside her and hold her in my arms, letting her cry against my blouse, her head tucked beneath my chin.

As I look to Brant, he gives me a reassuring nod.

Thinking about all the times we missed, all those milestones and firsts, fills my marrow with weighted sadness as I breathe her in, but looking toward the future and thinking about all the memories we're going to make fills me with the kind of joy only a mother could know.

CHAPTER 49

Wren

"Wren," Brant calls for me from the kitchen. "Can you come in here for a second?"

I place my book aside and gently push Evie from my lap, where she's been lounging all day in pink pajamas covered in unicorns, watching cartoons about talking mice. Brant calls this "lounging." Nicolette says it's what people do on weekends and there's no shame in relaxing.

I think I could get used to this.

Evie's been a Gideon for almost a full week now, and so far, she seems to be settling in as expected. I overheard Dr. Pettigrew say younger children are more resilient and better able to handle change. She then called Evie a "poster child," though I'm unsure what that means.

Several reluctant steps bring me to the kitchen, where I find Brant holding his phone. He places it down, screen-side up, on the table.

"We've been contacted by someone," he says. "A family member of yours. And we just received confirmation that she's legitimate."

My palm flattens against my chest before my fingers inch up my neck. I rub my thumb along my collarbone, trying to imagine who it could be and trying not to get my hopes up.

"She'd like to talk to you," he says, his eyes glinting as he points to his phone. "I've got her number programmed into my phone. You can call her now, or you can call her another time, when you're ready."

Taking his warm phone in my hand, I take a seat at the table.

"I want to call her now," I say in spite of the hammering in my chest and the dampness filling my palms. I'm not sure if I can go another night with a hundred unanswered questions keeping me awake.

"Are you sure?" he asks.

I nod, and he reaches over, tapping his phone until a name—Katrina—and phone number appear against a white background.

"All ready for you. Just press the 'call' button," he says.

I clear my throat, take two breaths, and press the button before bringing the phone to my right ear.

Three long tones play, and then nothing.

"Hello?" a woman asks.

"Hello," I say. My heart whooshes in my ears.

"Wren." The woman's voice on the other end is so loud, I have to pull the phone away for a second. "Oh, my *gawd*!"

"I'm sorry. Who is this?" I ask.

Brant smiles, arms folded as he watches. He must be able to hear her.

"I'm your Aunt Trina," she says. She talks funny, each syllable exaggerated and drawn out. "I just knew this day would come. Oh. My. *Gawd.* I'm sorry. I don't mean to fuss and carry on, but you have no idea how long I've been prayin' for this moment. You know, I knew there was a reason the good Lord wanted me to do one of those Family Tree DNA tests."

She laughs in a way that makes me wonder if she's crying, too.

"Brant tells me you're looking for your momma and daddy," she says with a sigh that tells me not to get my hopes up. "Darlin', I don't know how to tell you this, but they perished, oh, about seventeen or so years back."

My eyes brim, and I turn so Brant can't see me.

"There was a car accident. Single car. Your daddy was driving. There were no witnesses, and by the time anyone came across them, they'd already passed away," she says, her voice stifled and broken. "But your car seat . . . your car seat was empty at the scene. The police think someone came along and took you for themselves. There are some real sick people out there." She clucks her tongue. "You might be able to Google the story. The media called you Baby Felicity. It was this big thing on the national news for quite some time."

"Felicity?" I ask. Suddenly hearing my given name provides a temporary distraction from the bad news.

"Oh, yes. That was your name. *Is* your name, rather. Felicity Hollingsworth," she says. "Anyway, it was impossible to find you, what with no witnesses, no evidence, no leads. But we never forgot you. Not for one minute. Still have your baby picture in a frame on my dresser. Taken it to every house I've ever lived in."

My Aunt Trina sounds sweet and full of life, a warm soul much like the blonde woman I remember.

"I'd love to meet you, Wren," she says. "Sooner the better. I'm down here in Dallas, Texas, but I could hop on the next flight to New York if you'd like me to?"

"I'd love you to," I say, tears drying as I wear a smile too strong to fight.

"Say, you ever seen a picture of your folks?" she asks.

"No."

"Soon as we hang up, I'm going to text one to this number. How about that? And then I'll bring a bunch of albums when I come visit."

"Please, I'd love that," I say, nodding though she can't see me.

"All right, well, again, I can't tell you how thrilled I am to know you're alive and well," she says. "And I'm just dyin' to meet you. Will be in touch soon."

Trina ends the call, and within thirty seconds, the first picture message comes through.

It's her.

It's the woman with the yellow hair.

That was my mother.

CHAPTER 50

NICOLETTE

"First-degree kidnapping," Brant says as he hangs up his phone. "Murder in the first."

"Davis's charges?" I ask, sliding into bed.

It's been nearly two weeks since the night we found our daughter, though it's still as vivid as if it all took place last night. Sometimes when I close my eyes, I can hear the wail of the sirens, see the flash of the red and blue lights against the side of his trailer. The image of our daughter's sleepy-yet-frightened face will forever be burned into my memory, I'm sure.

The first night we came home after leaving Evie at the hospital, Brant went from room to room, yanking down every picture of Davis, every childhood memento that so much as made him think of his brother.

I asked if he wanted to talk about it as he dumped a box of framed photos into the trash bin. He rested his hands on his hips, gave the garbage one last look, and shut the lid.

"I'm good," he said after that. "We have Hannah back. Nothing else matters."

And just like that, I had my sweet-natured, kindhearted, optimistic husband back.

I scoot closer to Brant's side of the bed, bunching the covers around me.

"Yep," he says. "May says Davis plotted the entire thing. When Maggie needed meds for Evie, he gave her tainted vitamins instead, ones he knew would make her sick enough she'd need medical attention. Guess Maggie had an emergency satellite phone. Called him that night they left, and he met them in the woods. Killed Maggie. Took Evie."

"So how did he know that Evie was ours?" I ask. "And how long did he know?"

"Only recently. Maybe less than a year? He claims Maggie told him a lot of things, and he began to piece them together," he says. "She trusted him. Guess he used to work with her husband at the factory before he died."

"So . . . what was he planning to do with Evie?"

Brant shrugs. "Honestly, I think he was planning to extort us for as long as he could."

Davis has never been a man with any long-term direction. He's never had his sights set on the future. I doubt he thought that far ahead. The idiot probably thought he could milk us indefinitely.

"At least he didn't hurt her," I say.

"He's a lot of things, but I don't think he's got it in him to hurt an innocent child, let alone his own flesh and blood."

I decide not to tell Brant that I disagree. If his brother was capable of extortion and keeping Evie away from us for his own gain, he was capable of anything. For now, I want to focus on the positive, on moving forward so we can all heal and put ourselves back together.

"Mom and Dad are coming this weekend. They can't wait to meet her," I say. "And Wren, too."

Wren's just as much a part of our family now. I spent an hour last night on the phone with my mother, telling her how much she was going to love Wren. Going on about her resiliency and her intelligence and how proud I was of her for staying so strong and fearless through all this.

"You speak of her as if she's your own daughter," my mother said toward the end of our talk.

I lay awake most of last night, trying to imagine what our future will look like from here on out, and every scenario has one thing in common: Wren is a part of them.

For nine years, Wren has loved Evie, looked after her, kept her safe. The least I can do is to give her the gift of knowing Evie will forever and always be her sister and the security of knowing she's welcome to stay here, with us, as a part of our family.

"Can we adopt her?" I ask. "I know she's almost twenty, but we can still do that, right? If she wants us to?"

There are a million things we need to focus on: getting to know Evie, ensuring she's adjusting, reaching a point where she's comfortable enough to call us something besides our given names, but there's a niggle at the center of my heart that aches for Wren when I think about what comes next for her. Whatever it is, I want us to be a part of it.

Brant slides in beside me, leaning over to steal a kiss. "We can, and we should."

CHAPTER 51

Wren

Six Months Later

Six days.

That's how long we have until we leave for Miami. Brant and Nic are taking us to visit their friend Cate.

I drag a black *X* across today's date on the clear plastic calendar hanging on the side of the refrigerator. A pink heart circles the last day of this month—the adoption hearing with a family court judge. The Gideons insisted on adopting me despite my being a legal adult, and they wanted to "go through the proper channels," which involved meetings with people in suits and mountains of papers to sign. I told them they didn't have to do this, but they insisted, saying any family of Evie's was family of theirs.

It was only when I found myself hugging the two of them that I realized how much I wanted to be a part of their family. We'd grown so close, so fast, and they've been so good to me, helping me navigate my new life and teaching me about things I never knew existed before. And besides, I couldn't imagine leaving Evie.

Nicolette said it's hot in Florida this time of year, that we won't need a ton of clothes. And Brant said we'll probably spend most of our time swimming or combing the beach for beautiful shells. He promised to teach us how to swim as soon as we get there.

Evie can't wait. Brant showed her a video of what swimming is, and now it's all she talks about. Actually, anything Brant shows her or teaches her is all she can talk about. She's his shadow, following him everywhere, always wanting to see what he's doing, always asking a thousand questions. The other night, I overheard Nicolette telling Brant she loved how patient he was with Evie. He told her waiting nine years to hold your daughter again makes being patient easy.

Brant snaps photos of me marking the calendar. I didn't see him standing there. He does that a lot—takes what he calls "candid shots." He says the pictures are better that way, and he tells us just to pretend he's not there anytime we see him with his camera. Nicolette says he's working on some family series for his next exhibit and that we're going to take a trip to Berlin, Germany, next year so we can see his work on display in an art museum.

It's a strange little family we make, but for the first time in my life, I'm home.

ACKNOWLEDGMENTS

A million thank-yous to the following individuals who worked hard behind the scenes to make this book happen: Jill Marsal, Jessica Tribble, and Charlotte Herscher. Thank you for your top-notch professionalism and ongoing support and encouragement.

To my betas: Pamela Hull, Deanna Finn, and Ashley Cestra. This book wouldn't be what it is without your relentless passion for reading, savvy suggestions, and eyes for detail.

To Chuck, Max, Kat, Marin, and Jennifer, my circle of brilliant, talented, and trusted authors whom I'm fortunate to also call friends. Thank you for letting me celebrate, vent, and bounce ideas off you, and for being like virtual colleagues I can bother when I'm "on break."

To my husband and kids, thank you for never making me feel guilty when deadlines are looming and my work-life balance is completely unfair. You're my rock, my world, and my everything.

ABOUT THE AUTHOR

Photo © 2017 Jill Austin Photography

Washington Post bestselling author Minka Kent is the author of *The Thinnest Air*; *The Perfect Roommate*; *The Stillwater Girls*; and *The Memory Watcher*, which has been optioned by NBCUniversal. She is a graduate of Iowa State University and resides in Iowa with her husband and three children. For more information, visit www.minkakent.com or www.facebook.com/authorminkakent.